Ben stood there for a minute looking at her. Don't do it, he told himself. She wasn't ready to have her world rattled. She wasn't ready for a man like him. There was no sense complicating things between them.

But as it turned out, Beth made the choice, not him. Just as he turned to go out the door he felt her hand, feather-light, on his shoulder. He turned back, and it was she who stood on her tiptoes and brushed her lips against his.

It was like tasting cool, clean water after years of drinking water gone brackish. It was innocence in a world of cynicism. It was beauty in a world that had been ugly. It was a glimpse of a place he had never been.

So the truth was not that she was not ready for a man like him. The truth was that he was not ready for a woman like her.

Who would require so much of him. Who would require him to learn his whole world all over again. Who would require him to be so much more than he had ever been before.

Dear Reader,

As I write, it is fall in Canada—a gorgeous season of vibrant color, cold nights and sunshine-filled days. Yesterday I rode my Appaloosa, Dakota, on a winding forest trail, the leaves crunching under his feet, the crisp, clean aroma of fall in the air. I was so aware that this experience of total connection, of intense engagement with my senses and my surroundings, was becoming part of who I am and what I bring to the world. I was drawing this perfect experience deep within me as a source of energy and inspiration to tap during the long months of winter.

Everyone has something that makes them feel all will be right in a mixed-up world. Whether it is dancing or gardening, or curling up with a wonderful book, I encourage each of you to find that place that sends you back to your daily life rejuvenated and ready to take on the challenges of everyday life. I am deeply honored that some of you choose to do that through my stories.

With warmest wishes,

Cara

CARA COLTER
Miss Maple and the Playboy

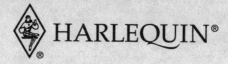

HARLEQUIN®

TORONTO • NEW YORK • LONDON
AMSTERDAM • PARIS • SYDNEY • HAMBURG
STOCKHOLM • ATHENS • TOKYO • MILAN • MADRID
PRAGUE • WARSAW • BUDAPEST • AUCKLAND

Recycling programs
for this product may
not exist in your area.

ISBN-13: 978-0-373-17604-5

MISS MAPLE AND THE PLAYBOY

First North American Publication 2009.

Copyright © 2009 by Cara Colter.

www.eHarlequin.com

Printed in U.S.A.

Cara Colter lives on an acreage in British Columbia with her partner, Rob, and eleven horses. She has three grown children and a grandson. She is a recent recipient of a *Romantic Times BOOKreviews* Career Achievement Award in the Love and Laughter category. Cara loves to hear from readers, and you can contact her, or learn more about her, through her Web site, www.cara-colter.com.

Don't miss Christmas with Cara Colter
in her next Harlequin Romance

Snowbound Bride-to-Be

December 2009

To Chris Bourgeois,
aka riding buddy, drifter, equine therapist

CHAPTER ONE

"IT SUCKS to be you."

Ben Anderson opened his mouth to protest and then closed it again. He contemplated how those few words summed up his life and decided the assessment was not without accuracy. Of course, the truth of those words was closely linked to the fact he had become guardian to the boy who had spoken them, his eleven-year-old nephew, Kyle.

It was a position Ben had held for precisely ten days, the most miserable of his life, which was saying quite a bit since he had spent several years in the Marine Corps, including an eight-month tour of duty in the land of sand and blood and heartbreak.

At least over there, Ben thought, there had been guidelines and rules, a rigid set of operating standards. Becoming Kyle's guardian was like being dropped in the middle of a foreign country with no backup, no map, and only a rudimentary command of the language.

For instance, did he tell Kyle he was sick of the expression *It sucks to be you* or did he let it pass?

While contemplating his options, Ben studied the

envelope in front of him. It was addressed to Mr. Ben Anderson and in careful brackets Kyle's Guardian just so that where was no wriggling out of it. The handwriting was tidy and uptight and told Ben quite a bit about the writer, though Kyle had been filling him in for the past ten days.

Miss Maple, Kyle's new teacher at his new school was old. And mean. Not to mention supremely ugly. "Mugly," Kyle had said, which apparently meant more than ugly.

She was also unfair, shrill-voiced and the female re-incarnation of Genghis Khan.

Kyle was a surprising expert on Genghis Khan. He'd informed Ben, in a rare chatty moment, that a quarter of the world's population had Khan blood in them. He'd said it hopefully, but Ben doubted with Kyle's red hair and freckles that his nephew was one of them.

Ben flipped over the envelope, looking for clues. "What does Miss Maple want?" he asked Kyle, not opening the letter.

"She wants to see you," Kyle said, and then repeated, "It sucks to be you."

Then he marched out of his uncle's kitchen as if the fact that his old, mean and ugly teacher wanted to see his uncle had not a single thing to do with *him*.

Ben thought the responsible thing to do would be to call his nephew back and discuss the whole "it sucks" thing. But fresh to the concept of being responsible for anyone other than himself, Ben wasn't quite sure what the *right* thing to do was with Kyle. His nephew had the slouch and street-hardened eyes of a seasoned con, but just below that was a fragility that made Ben debate whether the Marine Corps approach was going to be helpful or damaging.

And God knew he didn't want to do anymore damage. Because the hard truth was if it sucked to be someone in this world, that someone was Kyle O. Anderson.

Ben's parents had been killed in a car accident when he was seventeen. He'd been too old to go into the "system" and too young to look after his sister, who had been fourteen at the time. Ben went to the marines, Carly went to foster care. Ben was well aware that he had gotten the better deal.

By the time she'd been fifteen, Carly had been a boiling cauldron of pain, sixteen she was wild, seventeen she was pregnant, not that that had cured either the pain or the wildness.

She had dragged Kyle through broken relationships and down-and-out neighborhoods. When Ben had been overseas and helpless to do a damn thing about it, she and Kyle had gone through a homeless phase. But even after he'd come back stateside, Ben's efforts to try and help her and his nephew had been rebuffed. Carly saw her brother's joining up as leaving her, and she never forgave him.

But now, only twenty-eight, Carly was dying of too much heartbreak and hard living.

And Ben found himself faced with a tough choice. Except for Carly, his life was in as close to perfect a place as it had ever been. Ben owned his own business, the Garden of Weedin'. He'd found a niche market, building outdoor rooms in the yards of the upscale satellite communities that circled the older, grittier city of Morehaven, New York.

A year ago he'd invested in his own house, which he'd bought brand-new in the well-to-do town of Cranberry Corners, a community that supported his business and was a thirty-minute drive and a whole world away from the mean streets of the inner city that Kyle and Carly had called home.

Ben's personal specialty was in "hardscaping," which was planning and putting in the permanent structures like decks, patios, fireplaces and outdoor kitchens that made the backyards of Cranberry Corners residents superposh. It was devilishly hard work, which suited him to a T because he was high energy and liked being in good shape. The business had taken off beyond his wildest dreams.

Ben also enjoyed a tight network of buddies, some of whom he'd gone to high school with and who enjoyed success and the single lifestyle as much as he did.

Did he disrupt all that and take sucks-to-be-him Kyle O. Anderson, with his elephant-size chip on his shoulder, or surrender him to the same system that had wrecked Carly?

Since Ben considered himself to be a typical male animal, self-centered, insensitive, superficial—and darned proud of it—he astonished himself by not feeling as if it was a choice at all. He felt as if sometimes a man had to do what a man had to do, and for him that meant taking his nephew.

Not that either his nephew or his sister seemed very appreciative.

Not that that was why he had done it.

Ben opened the tidy envelope from Miss Maple. He read that Kyle's behavior was disrupting her class, and that she needed to meet with him *urgently*.

Ben decided if Miss Maple had a plan for dealing with Kyle's behavior, he was all for it. Having decided against the drill-sergeant method, since it was untested on eleven-year-olds who were facing personal tragedy, Ben was at a loss about how to deal with the mouthiness, the surliness, the belligerence of his eleven-year-old nephew. There always seemed to be an undertow of hostility from Kyle.

Unfortunately, the note said he was supposed to meet with the much maligned Miss Maple fifteen minutes ago.

"Kyle?" he called down the hallway. There was no answer, and Ben went down the hall to Kyle's room.

He stood in the doorway for a moment. The room used to be Ben's home gym, complete with a wall-mounted TV and a stereo system with surround-sound speakers. Now all his workout stuff was in the basement, though he'd left the TV and stereo for Kyle.

Kyle was sprawled on the unmade bed. Highly visible were the cowboy sheets Ben had bought for him, along with the new twin-size bed, when he'd confirmed his nephew was coming to stay for good.

Kyle, naturally, had glared at the sheets and proclaimed them "for babies." Ben could see his point, as at the moment he was listening to ominous-sounding music in a foreign language and flipping the pages on a book with a title that looked like it might be Greek.

"When did your teacher give you this note for me?"

Kyle shrugged with colossal indifference.

"Not today?" Ben guessed dryly.

"Not today," Kyle agreed.

Ben glanced at his watch and sighed. "Let's go see Miss Maple," he said. "We're late."

"Miss Maple hates *tardiness*," Kyle said, obviously mimicking his teacher's screechy voice. He sounded quite pleased with himself that he had managed to get Ben in trouble with the teacher before they had even met.

Ben felt uneasily like a warrior going into the un-expected as he held open the door of Cranberry Corners Elementary School, and then followed Kyle down the highly polished floor of a long hallway. Was he going into battle, or negotiations? Strange thoughts for a man traveling down hallways lined with cheerful drawings of smiling suns and stick people walking dogs.

He stopped, just outside the doorway of the class Kyle pointed to, and frowned at what he saw inside. A woman sat at a lonely desk at the front of the class, mellow September sunshine cascading over her slender shoulders.

"That can't be Miss Maple."

Kyle peered past him. "That's her, all right."

It was because he'd been expecting something so radically different that the first sight of Miss Maple made Ben feel as if he had laid down his weapons somewhere. He felt completely disarmed by the fact that it was more than evident that not one thing Kyle had said about her was true. Or at least not the "mugly" or "old" part. He'd have to wait and see about the "mean." And the screechy voice.

There was something disarming about the classroom, too. A huge papier-mâché tree sprouted in one corner, the branches spreading across the ceiling, dripping with brightly colored fall leaves with kids' names on them. The wall contained charts full of shining stars, artwork, reprints of good paintings. This was the space of some-one who loved what she did. From Kyle's attitude, Ben had pictured something grimmer and more prisonlike for Miss Maple's lair.

But then, Miss Maple was not the Miss Maple he had imagined, either, and Ben struggled to readjust to the picture in front of him. In fact, the teacher was young, not more than twenty-five. She was concentrating on something on her desk, and her features were fine and flawless, her skin was beautiful, faintly sun-kissed, totally unlined. Her hair, pulled back in a ponytail, was the exact dark golden color of the wildflower honey that Ben kept in a glass jar on his countertop.

Of course, she could still be mean. Ben had known plenty of gorgeous women who were mean straight through. You could tell by their eyes, diamond flint and ice.

But then she lifted her eyes, and he was momentarily lost in their softness and their color, an astounding mix of jade and aqua and copper.

Nothing mean in those eyes, he decided, and tried out his best easygoing boy-next-door grin on her.

An unexpected thing happened. She frowned. It didn't make her look *mean* precisely, but he understood perfectly how an eleven-year-old boy could be intimidated by her.

"Hello," she said, "I think you must be lost." Her voice wasn't screechy at all. It was quite amazing, with the bell-like tone of a church bell ringing on a cold, pure morning. She leaned back in her chair and folded her arms over her chest, as if she had suddenly reached the alarming conclusion she was alone in this end of the building.

Women weren't generally alarmed by him, but the fact she was here at five in the evening probably meant she was sheltered in some way. The atmosphere in the classroom really was a testament to no life. How long did it take to make a tree like that? She'd probably been in here all summer, cloistered away, working on it!

More's the pity, since Ben could clearly see her chest was delicately and deliciously curved, though it occurred to him it was probably some kind of sin to notice that about the grade-five teacher, and the fact that he had noticed probably justified the alarm in her eyes.

Or maybe that was nuns a man was not supposed to think manlike thoughts about.

Which she was dressed like, not that he was an expert on how nuns dressed, but he suspected just like that: high-buttoned blouse in pristine white, frumpy sweater in forgettable beige.

He would have liked a glimpse of her legs, since he was unfortunately curious about whether she was wearing a skirt or slacks, but the desk totally blocked his view.

He moved forward, leaned over the desk and extended his hand. He couldn't think of a way to lean over far enough to see her legs without alarming her more than she already was, so he didn't.

"I'm Ben Anderson, Kyle's uncle." He deliberately turned up the wattage of his smile, found himself wishing he had changed out of his work clothes—torn jeans with the knee out, his company T-shirt with Garden of Weedin' emblazoned across the front of it.

Miss Maple took his hand but did not return his smile. Any idea he had about holding her hand a little too long was dismissed instantly. Her handshake was chilly and brief.

"You are very late," she said. "I was about to leave."

Ben was astounded to find he felt, not like six foot

one of hard-muscled fighting machine, but like a chastened schoolboy. Out of the corner of his eye, he saw Kyle slide in the door, and roll his shoulders inward, as if he was expecting a blow. Ben found he didn't have the heart to blame his nephew for not giving him the note.

"Uh, well," he said charmingly, "you know. Life gets in the way."

She was not charmed, and apparently she did not know. "Kyle, will you go down to the library? I had Mrs. Miller order a copy of *The History of Khan* for you. She said she'd leave it on her desk."

"For me?" Kyle squeaked, and Ben, astonished by the squeak glanced at him. The hard mask was gone from his eyes, and his nephew looked like a little boy who was going to cry. A little boy, Ben thought grimly, who had seen far too few kindnesses in his life.

He was aware the teacher watched Kyle go, too, something both troubled and tender in her eyes, though when she looked back at him, her gaze was carefully cool.

"Have a seat, Mr. Anderson."

Miss Maple seemed to realize at about the same time as Ben there really was no place in that entire room where he could possibly sit. The desks were too small, and she had the one adult-size chair.

He watched a faint blush rise up her cheeks and was reluctantly enchanted. He decided to smile at her again. Maybe she was one of those women who *liked* the real-man look, dirt and muscles. He flexed his forearm just a tiny bit to see if she was paying attention.

She was, because her blush deepened and she took a sudden interest in shuffling some papers on her desk. She apparently forgot she'd invited him to sit down.

"Your nephew is a bit of dilemma, Mr. Anderson," she said in a rush, shuffling frantically to avoid further eye contact with his muscles.

"Ben," he offered smoothly, hoping she might give up her first name in return.

But she didn't. In fact, she stopped shuffling papers and pressed her lips together in a firm line, gazed at him solemnly and sternly, the effect of the sternness somewhat tempered by the fact she picked that moment to tuck a wayward strand of that honey-colored hair behind her ear.

Ben had the unexpected and electrifying thought that he would like to kiss her. He wasn't sure why. Maybe as a shortcut to the woman underneath that uptight outfit and the stern expression.

She was not the kind of woman he usually went for. And he was pretty sure she was not the kind of woman who usually went for him.

She was the kind of woman where there wouldn't be any kind of shortcuts at all. If a guy were to date her, it wasn't going to end in her backyard hot tub after midnight.

Not that Miss Maple would have a hot tub! He regarded her thoughtfully, trying to guess at her afterschool activities. Knitting, possibly. Bird-watching, probably. Reading, definitely.

No, she was not his type at all.

Which probably explained why he felt intrigued by her. He wasn't quite sure when he'd become so sick to death of the kind of women who were his type, though that covered a lot of ground from supersophisticated debutantes, to rowdy party-hearty girls, to experienced divorcees, to free-spirited and very independent career women. None of them intrigued him anymore, and hadn't for a long time. For a while nobody had noticed, but lately his buddies were looking at Ben's ability to go home alone as if he had contracted a strange disease that needed to be cured before it became contagious.

The demure little schoolteacher made Ben Anderson feel challenged, the first interest he had felt in what the guys cheerfully called "the hunt" for a long, long time. Or maybe, he told himself wryly, he was looking for a little diversion from his sucks-to-be-you life.

Whatever it was, he now had a secret agenda that was making it very hard to focus on what she was saying about Kyle.

A contract for Kyle to sign. With goals and challenges and rewards.

"Mr. Anderson," she said, ignoring his invitation to call him Ben. "Your nephew has been held back once and has dismal test scores. He won't do his homework, and he doesn't participate in class discussions. But I think he reads at a college level and with complete comprehension.

"If I implement this plan for him," Miss Maple continued sternly, "it is going to take a tremendous amount of work and commitment on my part. I need to know you will be backing me at home, and that you are willing to put in the same kind of time and commitment."

Ben had been around long enough to know he should be very wary of a woman who tossed around the word *commitment* so easily.

He threw caution to the wind. "Why don't we discuss your plan in a little more detail over dinner?" he asked.

Miss Maple looked completely uncharmed. In fact, she looked downright annoyed.

He felt a little annoyed himself. Women didn't generally look annoyed when he asked them out for dinner. Delighted. Intrigued. He thought he should be insulted that the fifth-grade teacher didn't look the least delighted about his invitation or the least intrigued by him.

She was probably trying to be professional, trying to backpedal since he had seen her blush when he'd flexed his muscle. She wasn't as immune as she wanted him to think.

"I'm afraid I don't go for dinner with parents," Miss Maple said snippily.

Despite the fact he was amazed by her rejection, Ben assumed an expression that he hoped was a fair approximation of complete innocence. "Miss Maple," he chided her, "I am not Kyle's parent. I'm his uncle."

There was the little blush again, but Ben was almost positive it was caused by irritation, not the flexing of his forearm.

"I don't date the family members of my students," she said tightly, spelling it out carefully.

"Date?" Ben raised a surprised eyebrow. "You misunderstood me. I wasn't asking you on a date."

Now she had the audacity to look faintly hurt!

The problem with a woman like Miss Maple, Ben thought, was that she would be way more complicated than the women he normally took out. Challenge or not, he knew he should cut his losses and run for the door.

Naturally, he did nothing of the sort.

"I just thought we could get together and go over your plan in more detail." Ben looked at his watch. "Kyle hasn't eaten yet, and I'm trying to get him into regular meals."

That was actually true. His nephew was alarmingly

small and skinny for his age, a testament to the Bohemian lifestyle Carly had subjected him to. At first he had resisted Ben's efforts to get him to eat good food at regular intervals, but in the last few days Ben thought he noticed his nephew settling into routines, and maybe even liking them a bit.

He found himself sharing that with Miss Maple, who looked suitably impressed.

"He's had it tough, hasn't he?" she whispered.

Ben could see the softening of the stern line of her face. It made her look very cute. *Time to pounce.* If he asked her for dinner again right now, she'd say yes.

But he was surprised to find he couldn't. Instead he could barely speak over the lump that had developed in his throat. He couldn't even begin to tell her just how tough that kid had had it.

Even though he knew he was capable of being a complete snake, Ben found he could not use Kyle's tragic life to get what he wanted.

Which was a date with Miss Maple. Just to see how it would end. But he'd leave it for now because, whatever else he might be, he had a highly developed sense of what was fair. She genuinely cared about Kyle. That was obvious. And nothing to be played with, either. His nephew had had few enough people care about him without his uncle jeopardizing that in search of something as easy to find as a date with an attractive member of the opposite sex.

Yes, he needed to think the whole thing through a little more carefully.

So, naturally, he didn't. He found himself giving her his cell-phone number, just in case she needed to consult with him during the day. At least that was putting the ball in her court.

She took it, but reluctantly, as if she sensed what he really wanted to consult with her about was her after-school activities.

Kyle came back in the room, clutching his new book to his chest.

"How long can I keep it?" he demanded rudely.

"It's yours," Miss Maple said gently. "I ordered it just for you."

Kyle glared at her. "I've read it before. It's stupid. I don't even want it."

Ben had to bite back a desire to snap at his nephew for being so ungrateful for the kindness offered, but when he looked at Miss Maple, she was looking past the words, to the way Kyle was hugging the book. She said, not the least ruffled, "You keep it anyway. Your uncle might enjoy it."

Ben looked at her sharply, to see if there was a barb buried in the fact Miss Maple thought he might enjoy a stupid book, but nothing in her smooth expression gave her away.

He felt that little flutter of excitement again. He recognized it as a man with a warrior spirit exploring brand-new territory, where there was equal opportunities for success or being shot down.

"I like the tree," Ben said, thinking, *Flattery will get you everywhere*.

"Thank you," she said. "We made it last year as our class project."

It must have shown on his face that he thought that was a slightly frivolous use of school time, because she said haughtily, "We use it as a jumping-off point for all kinds of learning experiences in science, math and English. 'What is learned with delight is never forgotten.' Aristotle."

After they left the school, Ben took Kyle for a burger.

"Your teacher didn't seem that old to me," he said. Of all the things he could have picked to talk about, why her? A woman who quoted Aristotle. With ease. Whoo boy, he should be feeling warned off, not intrigued.

Kyle didn't even look at him, he was so engrossed in his new book. "That's because you're not eleven."

Leave it. There were all kinds of ways to make conversation with an eleven-year-old. *How about those Giants?*

"She didn't seem all that ugly, either."

The burgers had arrived, and Kyle was being so careful not to get stains on his new book that he barely would touch his dinner.

"Well, you haven't seen her face when you don't hand in the homework assignment."

"It would be good if you handed in the homework assignments," Ben said, thinking Kyle was lucky to have a teacher who was so enthusiastic and who actually cared. He remembered "the plan." "If you do it for a month without missing, I'll get us tickets to a Giants game."

Kyle didn't even look up from his book.

On the way home they stopped in at the hospital to see Carly, but she was sleeping, looking worn and fragile and tiny in the hospital bed. Pretty hard to interest a kid whose mom was that sick in a Giants game, Ben thought sadly. Still, he didn't know how to comfort his nephew, and he felt the weight of his own inadequacy when they got home and Kyle went right to his room without saying good-night and slammed his bedroom door hard. Moments later Ben heard the ominous sounds of a musical group shouting incomprehensibly.

He suddenly felt exhausted. His thoughts drifted to Miss Maple and he didn't feel like a warrior or a hunter at all.

He felt like a man who was alone and afraid and who had caught a glimpse of something in the clearness of those eyes that had made him feel as if he could lay his weapons down and fight no more.

The Top-Secret Diary of Kyle O. Anderson

Once, when I was little, my mom told me my uncle Ben was a lady-killer. When she saw the look on my face after she said it, she laughed and said it didn't mean he killed ladies.

It meant women loved him. Now that I live with him, I can see it's true. Whenever we go anywhere, like the burger joint tonight, I see women look at my uncle like he is the main course and they would like to eat him up. They get this funny look in their eyes, the way a little kid looks at a puppy, as if they are already half in love, and they haven't even talked to him.

I know where that look goes, too, because I've seen it on my mom's face, and I'm old enough to know simple problem math. Love plus my mom equals disaster. It probably runs in the family.

I like diaries. I have had one for as long as I can remember after I found one my mom had been given and never used. It had a key and everything. Having a diary is like having a secret friend to tell things to when they get too big to hold inside. I stole the one I am using now because it has a key, too, and I didn't want anyone to laugh at me when I bought it, though afterward I felt bad, and thought I could have said I was buying it for my older sister for her birthday. Which is a lie because I don't have an older sister. I wonder which is a worse bad thing, telling a lie or stealing?

There's lots of things people don't know about me, like I don't really like to do bad things, but it kind of keeps anyone from guessing that I'm so scared all the time that my stomach hurts.

My mom is going to die. She weighs about ninety pounds now, less than me, and I can see bones and blue veins sticking out on her hands. There's a look in her eyes, like she's saying goodbye, even though she still talks tough and as if everything's going to be okay and she's coming home again. Anybody, even a kid, can see that that's not true.

Not that I feel like a kid most of the time. I feel like I've been looking after my mom way longer than she's been looking after me.

Not that I did a very good job of it. Look at her now.

My mom is not like the moms in movies or storybooks. She drinks too much and likes to party, and she falls in with really creepy people. Her boyfriend right now is a loser named Larry. He doesn't even go visit her in the hospital unless her welfare cheque has come and he needs it signed. Uncle Ben moved her to the hospital closer to us, so, gee, Larry would have to take the bus and transfer twice. At least he never hit her or me, which is different than the last one, who was a loser named Barry. That is the sad poem of my mom's life.

Here is another secret: even though I am scared of her

dying, I am scared of her living, too. I try not to let my uncle know, but I like it at his house. It's not just that it's nice, even though it is, it's that everything is clean, and he always has food, even if it's dorky stuff like bananas and apples and hardly any cookies or potato chips.

I feel safe here, like I know what's going to happen next, and there aren't going to be any parties in the middle of the night where people start screaming at each other and breaking bottles and pretty soon you hear the sirens coming.

It's weird because one of the things I'm scaredest of is that my uncle won't like me. What will happen to me if he sends me away? And even though that makes me so scared I want to throw up, I am really mean to him. My mom was always mean to him, too. Whenever he turned up, even though he always had groceries for us, she'd yell at him to get lost and it was too late and we didn't need him, and then as soon as he left, she'd slam the door behind him and say, "Why can't he ever say he loves me," and cry for about a week. Which is kind of how I feel after I'm mean to him, too.

He bought all new stuff for my room at his house, and he let me have his supercool TV set and stereo. I never had new stuff before—a brand-new bed and sheets that were so new they felt scratchy the first night I slept in them. It made me want to cry that he bought them just for me, and that he left the television set in there, even though he doesn't even have one in his own bedroom. It kind of made me hope maybe I was staying for good, but I am old enough to know that hope is the most dangerous thing. Maybe that's why I acted mad instead, and told him how lame the cowboy were.

My uncle Ben used to be a marine. He's big as a mountain, and he's probably killed all kinds of people. Maybe with his bare hands. I can't be a crybaby around him.

At my new school everything is new and shiny, and you don't have to go through a metal detector at the front door. The library has lots of books in it, but I'm trying not to care about that too much, either, in case everything changes. You don't want to put too much faith in a place with a corny name like Cranberry Corners. It's not even real. Do you see any cranberries around here?

It is the same with Miss Maple, like she is too good to be true. She does really nice things for me, like the book tonight, but it makes me wish I was little and could just climb on her lap and cry and cry and cry. See? There's that crybaby thing again.

Have you ever seen those movies where people live in a big house on a nice block, with a golden retriever and the kind of yard my uncle builds? All flowers and fountains and that kind of stuff?

Miss Maple is the mom in that movie. You can tell by looking at her, when she gets married and has kids there will be no parties where things get smashed in the night!

No sirree, she will have baked cookies and would serve them warm with milk before bed. And then a nice bath, every single night, whether you are dirty or not, and then I bet she would get right in bed with her kid and read him stories about something lame like turtles that talk.

She would have stupid rules like brushing your teeth, and saying please and thank you and not being *tardy,* and that's why I act like I hate her, because she is the mom I wanted and sure didn't get, and I feel guilty for thinking that when my own mom is going to die.

I told my uncle she was old and mean and ugly because it would have been so much easier for me if that's what she had been. Plus him being a lady-killer and all, I didn't want him to ever get anywhere near her. Because who knows what would happen next?

I like knowing what is going to happen next. Even though it is supergross to think of your uncle and your teacher *liking* each other, I had an ugly feeling that it was a possibility. I am always thinking of possibilities, trying really hard not to be surprised by life.

I guess I should never have given him the note from her, because it was worse than I imagined when they saw each other. I know *that* look. It usually happens just when my life is getting good, too. Just me and my mom, then *that* look between her and the latest loser and it's a straight downhill slide from there. Not that my uncle or Miss Maple are losers, but I still think if it runs in the family, I'm doomed.

I can probably scare her off my uncle. Sheesh. He comes with a kid. The most rotten kid in her class. She's no dummy. She can do math, too. But what if he decides to have her and get rid of me?

This is the kind of question that makes my stomach hurt. I will just keep her from ever wanting to get mixed up with us.

I wonder if Miss Maple will scream if I put a frog in her desk?

I saw one, a really big one, at Migg's Pond, which is behind the school and out of bounds, except for the science-class field trip. We didn't go on field trips in my old school.

And just thinking about that, how to capture that frog, instead of my mom lying alone in a hospital, and whether or not my uncle is going to keep me, or whether my uncle and Miss Maple are going to progress to the making-eyes-at-each-other stage, eases the ache in my stomach enough that I can go to sleep, finally.

But only if I leave the light on.

CHAPTER TWO

BETH Maple heard a slightly muffled snicker just as she was sliding open her top desk drawer looking for a prize for Mary Kay Narsunchuk, who had just won the weekly spelling bee.

During the whole spelling bee, out of the corner of her eye, Beth had seen Kyle O. Anderson looking absently out the window, seeming not to pay attention, unaware his mouth was silently forming every letter of every word she had challenged the class with, including the one that had finally stumped Mary Kay, *finesse*. But every time she had called on him to spell a word, Kyle had just frowned and ducked his head.

It was an improvement over last week's spelling bee. Whenever she had called on Kyle that time, he had spelled a word, all right, but never the word he'd been given. When the word was *tarry*, he spelled *tarantula*, when she gave him *forte*, he spelled, or started to spell *fornication*. She had cut him off before he'd completed the word. Thankfully, no one in her grade-five class seemed to have any idea what that exchange had been about.

But Kyle was being suspiciously well-behaved for

this spelling bee. At her most optimistic she hoped that meant his uncle had talked to him after their meeting last night about the plan, and had implemented the reward system at home.

It was probably that momentary lapse, thinking about Kyle's uncle, that made Beth react slowly to the snicker as she was opening her desk drawer. Her brain shouting "Beware" did not get to her hand in time. Of course, her brain could just as well have been warning her off the gorgeous, full-of-himself, Ben Anderson, as the contents of her desk drawer!

A blob of green exploded from the desk, and collided with her hand, unbelievably *squishy* and revolting. Beth did what no grade-five teacher should ever do.

She screamed, then caught herself and stuffed her fist in her mouth. She regarded the largest frog she had ever seen, which sat not three feet in front of her on the floor, glaring at her with beady reptilian eyes.

It's only a frog, she told herself sternly, but nevertheless she screamed again when it leaped forward. She could hear Kyle's satisfied chortles above all the other sounds in a classroom that was quickly dissolving into pandemonium.

Twelve economy-size knights rushed to rescue their teacher, aka damsel-in-distress, though she was not naive enough to believe chivalry had trumped the pure temptation of the frog.

Casper Hearn led the charge, a big boy, throwing desks and hysterical girls out of his way as he stampeded around the room in pursuit of the frog.

But somehow, out of the melee, it was Kyle who emerged, panting, the frog clutched to his chest. Now he faced the other boys, something desperate in his pinched, pale face as they surrounded him. His freckles were standing out in relief he was so white.

"Give me the frog," Casper ordered Kyle with distinct menace.

"I'll warn you once to stay away from me," Kyle said, a warning that might have been more effective if his voice wasn't shaking and Casper didn't outweigh him by a good thirty pounds.

Casper laughed. "Is that so? Then what?"

"Then the aisles will run with the fat melting from your bodies!" Kyle shouted, slipping the frog inside his shirt.

Casper took a startled step back from Kyle. The classroom became eerily silent. Casper stared at Kyle, shook his head and then went and sat down, followed by the other boys.

Kyle gave Beth a look she interpreted as apologetic and darted out the door, Kermit happily ensconced in his shirt.

When he didn't return, she realized with a horrible sense of resignation she was going to have to inform Kyle's uncle she had lost his nephew.

And the truth was, Beth Maple would have been just as happy if she never had to speak to Ben Anderson again.

Or at least the part of her that hadn't nearly swooned from the pure and powerful presence of the man would be happy.

The other part, despicably weak, yearned for just one more peek at him.

Beth thought that Ben Anderson was the type of man who should have a warning label on him. There was that word again. *"Beware."* Followed by *"Contents too potent to handle."*

She did not think she had ever been around a man who was so casually and extraordinarily sexy. When he had walked into her room yesterday, it was as if everything but him had faded to nothing. No wonder she had thought he was in the wrong place, hopelessly lost amongst the welcoming fall leaves that dripped from her ceiling and brushed the top of his head.

Ben Anderson was all masculine power. Every single thing about him, from the ease with which he held that amazing male body, to the cast of features made more mesmerizing by the fact his once-perfect nose had the crook of a break in it, radiated some kind of vital male energy.

He oozed strength and self-assurance, from the ripple of muscle, to the upward quirk of a sexy lip. But somehow all that self-assurance was saved from becoming arrogance by the light that danced in eyes as green as a summer swimming hole. Ben Anderson's eyes were warm and laughter filled. Kyle's propensity for mischief was undoubtedly genetic.

Still, something lurked behind the easy laughter of his eyes, the upward quirk of that sexy mouth. There was an untouchable place in Ben Anderson that was as remote as a mountaintop. But unfortunately, rather than making him less attractive, it intrigued, added to a kind of sizzling sensuality that tingled in the air around him.

Ben Anderson had that certain indefinable something that made women melt.

And he knew it, too, the scoundrel.

Beth, sharing her classroom with him last evening, had been totally aware she was an impossibly unworldly grade-five teacher, with nothing at all in her experience to prepare her for a man like that.

You didn't meet a man like Ben Anderson on the university campus. No, his type went to high, lonely places and battlefields. Even if Kyle had not mentioned to Beth that his uncle had been a marine, she would have known he had *something* other men did not have. It was in the warrior cast in his face, and the calm readiness in the way he carried himself.

He was not the kind of man she met at the parent-teacher conference, the kind who had devoted himself to a wife and children and a dream of picket fences. She met the occasional single dad, attractive in an expensive charcoal-gray suit, but never anything even remotely comparable to Ben Anderson.

Ben's eyes resting on her face had made her feel as if an unwanted trembling, pre-earthquake, had started deep inside of her.

She hated that feeling, of somehow not being in control of herself, which probably explained why she had been driven to explain the educational benefits of her classroom tree to him. And to quote Aristotle! Who did that to a man like him?

But Beth Maple loved being in control, and she especially loved it since her one crazy and totally uncharacteristic trip outside her comfort zone had left her humiliated and ridiculously heartbroken.

She had known better. She was the least likely person to ever make the mistake she had made. She was well educated. Cautious. Conventional. Conservative. But she had been lured into love over the Internet.

Her love, Rock Kildore, had turned out to be a complete fabrication, as if the name shouldn't have warned her. "Rock" was really Ralph Kaminsky, a fifty-two-year-old married postal clerk from Tarpool Springs, Mississippi. What he was not was a single jet-setting computer whiz from Oakland, California, who worked largely in Abu Dhabi and who claimed to have fallen hopelessly in love with a fifth-grade teacher. Even the pictures he'd posted had been fake.

But for a whole year, Beth Maple had believed what she wanted desperately to believe, exchanging increasingly steamy love letters, falling in love with being in love, anticipating that moment each day when she would open her e-mail and find Rock waiting for her. Beth had passed many a dreamy day planning the day all his work and travel obstacles would be overcome and she would meet the love of her life.

She had been so smitten she had *believed* his excuses, and been irritated by the pessimism of her friends and co-workers. Her mother's and father's concern had grated on her, partly because it was a relationship like theirs that she yearned for: stable but still wildly romantic even after forty years!

The youngest in her family, she hated being treated like a baby, as if she couldn't make the right decisions.

After her virtual affair had ended in catastrophe that was anything but virtual, Beth had retreated to her true nature with a vengeance. Most disturbing to her had been that underlying the sympathy of her mom and dad had been their disappointment in her. Well, she was disappointed in herself, too.

Now she had something to prove: that she was mature, rational, professional, quiet and controlled. These were the qualities that had always been hers—before she had been lured into an uncharacteristic loss of her head. They were the qualities that made her an exemplary teacher, and that she returned to with conviction.

Teaching would be enough for her. Her substantial ability to love would be devoted to her students now. Her passion would be turned on making the grade-five learning experience a delight worth remembering. And she was giving up on pleasing her parents, too, since they didn't seem any happier when she announced her choice to be single forever than they had been about Rock.

But looking at Ben Anderson, she had felt rattled, aware that all her control was an illusion, that if a man like that ever touched his lips to hers, she would surrender control with humiliating ease, dive into something hitherto wild and unexplored in herself.

Looking at Ben Anderson, Beth had thought, *No wonder I liked virtual love. The real thing might be too hot too handle!*

But even more humiliating than the fact Beth had recognized this shockingly lustful weakness in herself was the fact that she was almost positive he had recognized it in her, as well! There had been knowing in his eyes, in the little smile that tickled the firm line of his lips, in the fact his hand had touched hers just a trifle too long when he had passed her his business card with his cellphone number on it.

Ben Anderson had obviously been the conqueror of thousands of hearts.

And all of them left broken, too, Beth was willing to bet.

Not that she had let the smallest iota of any of that creep into her voice when she had spoken to him. She hoped.

When he had handed her his business card, just in case

she had needed to *consult* with him, she'd had the ugly feeling he expected her to find some pretext to use it.

And here she was, dialing his number, and hating it, even if this was a true emergency. And at the same time she hated it, a wicked little part of her was completely oblivious to the urgency of this situation, and wanted to hear his voice again, and compare it to her memory. No man could really sound that sexy.

Except he did.

His voice, when he answered, was deep and mesmerizing. Beth asked herself if she would think it was that sexy if she had never met him in person.

The answer was an unfortunate and emphatic yes.

There was a machine running in the background and Ben sounded faintly impatient, even when Beth said who she was and even though she could have sworn he would be pleased if she called him.

"Mr. Anderson, Kyle has gone missing."

"I can't hear you. Sorry."

"Kyle's gone," she screamed, just as the machine behind him shut off.

The silence was deafening, and she rushed to fill it, which was what a man like that did to a woman like her, took all her calm and measured responses and turned them on their head.

She explained the frog incident. Ben listened without comment. She finished with, "And then he ran off. I checked all the usual hideouts, under the stage in the gym, the last stall in the boy's washroom, the janitorial closet. I'm afraid he's not here."

"Thanks for letting me know," Ben said. "Don't worry."

And then Beth was left holding a dead phone, caught

between admiration for his I-can-handle-this attitude
when obviously he was fairly new and naive to the trouble little boys could get themselves into, and irritation
that somehow, just because he had told her not to worry,
she did feel less worried.

He was that kind of man. Ridiculous to plan picket
fences around him, and yet if you had your back against
the wall, and the enemy rushing at you with knives in
their teeth, he was the one you would want to be with you.

Beth told herself, sternly, it was absolutely idiotic to
think you could know that about a man from having seen
him once, and heard his supersexy voice on the phone.
But she knew it all the same. If the ship was sinking, he
would be the one who would find the life raft.

And the desert island.

She spent a silly moment contemplating that. Being
with Ben Anderson on a desert island. It was enough to
make her forget she had lost a child! It was enough to
remind her her ability to imagine things had gotten her
into trouble before.

An hour later, just as school was letting out and she
was watching the children swirl down the hallway in an
amazing rainbow of energy and color, the outside doors
swung open and Ben Anderson stood there, silhouetted
by light. He came through the children, the wave part-
ing around him, looking like Gulliver in the land of
little people.

There was something in his face that made Beth feel
oddly relieved, even though his expression was grim and
Kyle was not with him.

"Did you find him?" she asked.

The hallway was now empty. The absence of little

people did not make Ben Anderson seem any smaller. In fact, she was very aware that she felt small as she stood in his shadow.

Small and exquisitely feminine despite the fact she was wearing not a spec of makeup, her hair was pulled back in a no-nonsense bun and she was dressed exactly like the fifth-grade teacher that she was.

"Not yet. I thought he might be at home, but he wasn't." He was very calm, and that made her feel even more as if he was a man you could lean into, be protected by.

Without warning, his finger pressed into her brow. "Hey, don't worry, he's okay."

"How could you possibly know that?" she asked, aware that the certain shrill note in her voice had nothing to do with the loss of a child who had been in her charge, but everything to do with the rough texture of his hand pressed into her forehead.

"Kyle's eleven going on 102. He's been looking after himself in some pretty mean surroundings for a long, long time. He's okay."

He said that with complete confidence. He withdrew his hand from her forehead, looked at it and frowned, as though it had touched her without his permission. He jammed it in his pocket, and she felt the tiniest little thrill that the contact had apparently rattled him, as well as her.

"If he's not at home, where did he go?" she asked him. The news was full of all the hazards that awaited eleven-year-old boys who were not careful. In the week and a half that Kyle had been in her class, he had shown no sign that he was predisposed to careful behavior.

Of course, his uncle did not look as if he had ever been careful a day in his life, and he seemed to have survived just fine.

Probably to the woe of every female within a hundred miles of him.

"That's what I'm trying to figure out. Kyle's not that familiar with Cranberry Corners yet. Is he hiding somewhere? How much trouble does he think he's in?"

"It's not just about the frog," she told him, and repeated Kyle's awful remark.

"The aisles will run with the fat melting from your bodies?" Ben repeated. She couldn't tell if he was appalled or appreciative. "He said that?"

"Do you think he was threatening to burn down the school?" she whispered.

Ben actually laughed, which shouldn't have made her feel better, but it did. "Naw. He's a scrawny little guy. He used his brains to back down the bully, and it worked. Boy, where would he get a line like that?"

She was oddly relieved that it was not from his uncle!

"The History of Khan?" she guessed.

"Bingo!" he said, with approval for her powers of deduction.

She could not let herself preen under his approval. She couldn't. Wanting a man like him to approve of you could be the beginning of bending over backward to see that appreciative light in his eyes.

"Now if we could use those same powers of deduction to figure out where he is."

"You know him better than me," she said, backing away from the approval game. Besides, she really was drawing a blank about Kyle's whereabouts.

She saw the doubt cross his face, but he regarded her thoughtfully. "You said he still had the frog, right?"

She nodded.

"You said the other boys wanted the frog and he wouldn't give it to them."

Silly to be pleased that he had listened so carefully to what she had said. Troublesome how easily he could nudge down her defenses, even before they were rebuilt from the last collapse!

"So, let's assume he cared about the frog. Maybe he wanted to return it to where he got it from."

That made such perfect sense Beth wished she had thought of it herself.

"We went on a little field trip for science class last week. Migg's Pond," she said. "It's not far from here. We walked."

"I'm sure I can find it."

She was sure he could, too. But she was going with him. And not to spend time with him, either. Not because just standing beside him made her feel soft, and small and delicate.

She would go because this wasn't really about Ben nor her, nor even about a frog. It was about a child who, despite the fact he was street smart, was still a child. Somehow, someway, somebody needed to let him know that. That they would come for him when he had lost his way.

"I'll just get my jacket," she said. "And my boots." The boots were hideous, proof to herself that she was indifferent to the kind of impression she was making on Ben Anderson. No woman with the least bit of interest in how he perceived her would be seen dead in a skirt and gum boots by him.

"It's wet by the pond," she said, pleased with how rational she was being. She even leveled her grade-five-teacher look at his feet.

And then was sorry she had because her eyes had to travel the very long length of his hard-muscled legs to find the feet at the end of them.

"I'm not worried about getting my feet wet," he said, something flat in his voice letting her know that he had been in places and experienced things that made him scorn small discomforts.

Today Beth was wearing a plaid tartan skirt, which did not seem as pretty to her now as it had when she put it on this morning. The boots, unfashionable black rubbers with dull red toes, were kept in the coatroom for just such educational excursions. They looked hideous with her skirt, but since they were going to a swamp and she was determined to not try and impress him, she thought they were perfect for the occasion.

Still, when she saw the laughter light his eyes as she emerged from the coatroom, she wished she hadn't been quite so intent on appearing indifferent to his opinions. She wished she would have ruined her shoes!

In an effort not to look as rattled as she felt in her gum boot fashion disaster, she said conversationally, "I like the name of your business. Garden of Weedin'. Very original."

He glanced down at his shirt and grinned. A knowing grin, that accused her of studying his chest, which of course she had been.

"Very creative," she said stiffly, keeping on topic with stern determination as he held the door open for her to leave the school.

"Yeah, well, I stole it."

"What?"

"I saw it on a sign in a little town I was passing through a long time ago. It kind of stuck with me."

"I don't think you can steal names," she said. "That would be like saying my mother stole the name Beth from the aunt I was named after."

"Beth," he said, pleased, as if she had given away a secret he longed to know.

The way he said it made a funny tingle go up and down her spine. You could imagine a man saying your name like that, like a benediction, right before he kissed you. Or right before he talked you into his bed, the promise of bliss erasing the fact there had been the lack of a single promise for tomorrow.

She shot him a wary look, but he was looking ahead, scanning the terrain where the playground of the school met an undeveloped area behind it.

"Migg's Pond is out of bounds," she said. "The children aren't supposed to come back here by themselves."

He grunted. With amusement?

"Are you one of those people who scoffs at rules?" she asked.

"No, ma'am," he said, but his amusement seemed to be deepening.

"You are! I can tell."

"Now, how can you tell that?" he drawled, glancing at her with a lazy, sexy look that made her tingle just the way it had when he had spoken her name.

"I'm afraid I can picture you in fifth grade. Quite easily. Out of bounds would have just made it seem irresistible to you."

"Guilty."

"Frog in the teacher's drawer?" she asked.

"Only if I really liked her."

She contemplated that, and then said, "I don't think Kyle likes me at all."

"I would have, if I was in grade five. Not that I would have ever let on. How uncool would that be? To like the teacher."

How uncool would it be to feel flattered that a man would have liked you in grade five? It didn't mean he liked you now. Only a person without an ounce of pride would even pursue such a thing.

"What makes you think you would have liked me in grade five? I'm very strict. I think some of the kids think I'm mean."

He snorted, and she realized he was trying not to laugh.

"I am! I always start off the year at my most formidable."

"And I bet that's some formidable," he said, ignoring her glare.

"Because, you can't go back if you lose respect from the start. You can soften up later if you have to." She sounded like she was quoting from the teacher's manual, and Ben Anderson did not look convinced by how formidable she was capable of being!

"Well, I would have liked you because you were cute. And relatively young. And obviously you are into the Aristotle school of learning, which would mean really fun things like have everyone making a fall leaf with their name on it to hang from the roof."

He hadn't just used the tree to flatter her, which she had suspected at the time. He'd actually liked it. Why else would he have noticed details? She could not allow herself to feel flattered by that. *Weakened.*

He'd been a marine. He was probably trained to notice all the details of his environment.

They arrived at the pond. As she had tried to tell him, the whole area around it was muddy and damp.

But it wasn't him who nearly slipped and fell, it was her. She found his hand on her elbow, steadying her.

His grip, strong, sure, had the effect, *again,* of making her feel tiny and feminine. A lovely tingling was starting where his fingers dug lightly into her flesh.

She stopped and removed herself from his grip, moved a careful few steps away from him and scanned the small area around the pond with her best professional fifth-grade-teacher look.

As good as her intentions had been in coming here, and even though she had placed Kyle first, she had challenged herself as much as she intended to for one day.

"He's not here," she said. "I should go."

But Ben tilted his head, listening to something she couldn't hear. "He's here," he whispered.

She looked around. Nothing moved. Not even the grass stirred.

"How do you know?"

With his toe, he nudged a small sneaker print in the mud that she would have completely overlooked.

"It's fresh. Within an hour or so. So is this." His hand grazed a broken twig on a shrub near the pathway.

She didn't even want to know how he knew how fresh a print was, or a broken branch. She didn't want to know about the life he had led as a warrior, trained to see things others missed. Trained to shrug off hardship, go where others feared to go. Trained to deal with what came at him with calm and control. She didn't want to know all the multi-faceted layers that went into making such a self-assured man. Or maybe she did. Maybe she wanted to know every single thing about him that there was to know.

"Well," she said brightly, afraid of herself, her curiosity, terrified of the pull of him, "I'm sure you can take it from here. I'll talk to Kyle tomorrow."

"Okay," he said, scanning her face as if she didn't fool him one little bit, as if he knew how uncomfortable he made her feel, how aware of her *needs*.

"Are you going to follow the print?" she asked when he didn't move.

"I'd like him to come to us."

Us? She had clearly said she was leaving.

"Are you going to call him?" she asked.

"No. I'm going to wait for him. He knows we're here."

"He does?"

"Yeah."

She could go. Probably should go. But somehow she needed to put all her self-preserving caution aside, just for the time being. She needed to see this moment. Needed to be with the man who understood instinctively not to chase that frightened child, but to just wait. Or was that the pull of him, overriding her own carefully honed survival skills?

Ben took off his jacket, and put it on the soggy ground, patted it for her to sit on, just as if she had never said she was leaving, and just as if he had never said okay.

Something sighed in her, surrender, and she settled on his jacket, and he went down on his haunches beside her. Ben Anderson was so close she could smell his soap and how late-summer sunshine reacted to his skin.

"So," he said after a bit, "why don't you tell me something interesting about yourself?"

She slid him a look. This whole experience was suffused with an unsettling atmosphere of intimacy, and now he wanted to know something interesting about her? He had actually asked that as if he had not a doubt there was something interesting about her.

"What you consider interesting and what I consider interesting are probably two different things," she hedged.

"Uh-huh," he agreed. "Tell me, anyway."

And she realized he wanted Kyle to hear them talking, to hear that it was just a normal conversation, not about him, not loaded with anger or anxiety.

She suddenly could not think of one interesting thing about herself. Not one. "You first," she said primly.

"I like the ocean and warm weather," he said, almost absently, scanning the marshy ground, the reeds, the tall grass around Migg's Pond, not looking at her. "I like waves, and boats, swimming and surfing and deep-sea fishing. I like the moodiness of the sea, that it's cranky some days and calm others. I was stationed in Hawaii for a while, and I still miss it."

She tried not to gulp visibly. This was a little too close to her desert-island fantasy. She could picture him, with impossible clarity, standing at the water's edge, half-naked, sun and salt kissing his flawless body and his beautiful golden skin, white-foamed waves caressing the hard lines of his legs.

As if that vision had not made her feel weak with some unnamed wanting, he kept talking.

"I used to swim at night sometimes, the water black, and the sky black, and no line between them. It's like swimming in the stars."

"It sounds cold," she said, a pure defensive move against the picture he was painting, against the *wanting* unfurling within her like a limp flag in a gathering breeze.

"No," he said. "It's not cold at all. Even on colder days, the ocean stays about the same temperature year round. It's not warm like a bathtub, but kind of like—" he paused, thinking "—like silk that's been left outside in a spring breeze."

He did not look like a man who would know silk from flannel. But of course he would. The finest lingerie was made of silk, and no doubt he had worlds of experience with that.

"Parachutes," he said succinctly.

"Excuse me?"

"Made of silk."

As if it was that easy to read her mind! She hoped he wasn't going to ask her about her interesting experiences again. She had nothing at all to offer a man intimately familiar with night swimming, silk and jumping out of airplanes.

"Have you ever gone swimming in the dark, Beth?"

She hoped she was not blushing. This was totally unfair. Totally. She couldn't even sputter out a correction, that she wanted him to call her Miss Maple. Because she didn't. She wanted him to call her Beth, and she wanted to swim in the darkness. And run out and buy silk underwear. And maybe sign up for skydiving lessons while she was at it.

The problem with a man like him was that he could

make a person with a perfectly normal, satisfying life feel a kind of restless yearning for something more.

A restless yearning that had made her throw caution to the wind once before, she reminded herself. In her virtual romance with Rock, she had dared to embrace the unknown, the concept of adventure.

It had ended badly, and it would be worse if she let this man past her defenses, defenses which had seemed substantial until an hour ago.

Ben Anderson, conqueror of thousands of hearts, she reminded herself desperately. *Possibly more!*

"No," she managed to choke out. "I've never gone swimming in the dark." It felt like a confession, way too personal, desert-island confidences, not swamp exchanges.

"Too bad," he said, and looked at her, his pity real, as if it was written all over her she'd never swum in the dark.

She wondered, suddenly, horribly, if his nighttime swimming escapades had included swimming trunks.

Another thing she could add to the list of things she had never done, skinny-dipping. And would never do, either, if she had an ounce of self-respect!

Never mind that the thought of silk warm water on naked skin triggered some longing in her that was primal, dangerous and sensual.

"Though, I love to swim," she said. "We always had a pool."

"Ah, a pool," he said, as if that sounded tame indeed.

"Couldn't you have lived there?" she asked, wishing he had stayed there. "In Hawaii?"

"I guess I could have."

"Then why didn't you?" She didn't mean it to come

out as an accusation, but it did anyway. She felt as if her whole life could have remained so much safer and so much more predictable if he had made that choice. She certainly wouldn't be sitting here, longing for sensuality!

Buck up, she told herself sternly, *you can have a bubble bath when you get home.*

"I grew up here. My sister was here," he said, softly. "And Kyle."

She saw a nearby patch of rushes rustle, and realized Kyle had been that close all along, listening. He had heard every word. How had she missed that he was there?

Her eyes met the boy's. "Why, Kyle," she said. "There you are! We came here hoping to find you."

She hoped she had not spoken too soon, that he would not get up and bolt away, not ready to be found.

But Kyle stood up awkwardly and made his way over the slippery ground toward them. Which was a relief, not just because he was safe, and found, but because she didn't have to try and come up with something interesting to share with his uncle about herself.

As if she had anything that could compare to swimming in the dark in Hawaii!

Ben stood up then, and if he was affected by the long wait, crouched on his haunches, it did not show. Kyle came with no hesitation. Beth could see he was relieved to have been found, relieved his uncle was not angry with him. He had heard his uncle, and somehow his uncle had said exactly the right thing, exactly what that child needed to hear.

That someone had come back for him.

No man left behind.

Watching him watch his nephew, his gaze calm and

measured, she understood Ben Anderson was a man who knew instinctively how to get the job done and, more importantly, how to do the right thing. He was a man who trusted his instincts, and his instincts were good, sharp-honed by the fact that he, unlike most men she had met, had relied on his instinct, his gut, for his survival, and for the survival of his brothers.

If ever there was a child who needed that, it was Kyle.

But the sneaky appalling thought blipped, uninvited and uncensored through Beth Maple's brain, *And if ever a woman needed that, it is me.*

Wrong, she told herself. He was a man who could turn a swamp into a desert island. She was a woman who could turn a nonexistent person into her prince in shining armor.

She wasn't risking herself. She'd learned her lesson. She was sticking to teaching school, giving all her love to the children who came to her year after year.

A rather alarming picture of her in her dotage: alone, white hair in a crisp bun, marking papers with a cat on her lap crowded into her mind. But she pushed it away and jumped to her feet. The damp had seeped through the jacket Ben had set so chivalrously on the ground for her.

"Well," she said brightly, fighting an urge to swipe at her sodden rear end. "Child found. Emergency over. Goodbye." Totally unprofessional. She needed to discuss the events of the day with Kyle. There had to be consequences for putting the frog in her desk. For uttering the threat. For running away from school.

Instead she waggled her fingers ineffectually at Kyle, and made the mistake of looking once more at Ben.

He was looking at her with those sea-green amused eyes, a hint of a smile turning up his way-too-sexy mouth, and she turned briskly away from him and did not look back.

Because she knew his amusement would only deepen when he saw the condition of her dress, and she could not handle his amusement at her expense.

She could not handle him at all. He was a little too much of everything—too good-looking, too good with his instincts, too charming, even, stunningly, too poetic.

Her world was safe, and a man like that spelled one thing, danger.

"Hey, Beth?" he called after her.

She turned reluctantly, planning to tell him it was Miss Maple, especially in front of children, but somehow she couldn't. Somehow they had progressed beyond that, without her permission, when he had told her about swimming in the warm Pacific Ocean with the stars.

She hoped he wasn't going to remind her of her responsibilities, that they needed to deal with Kyle.

Oh, no, it was so much worse than that.

"You should have a bubble bath when you get home. It will take the chill off."

She was that transparent to him. He probably knew just how his tales of swimming in the dark had tugged at some secret place in her, too. She spun on the heel of her rubber boot so fast she nearly made her exit even more graceless than it already was by falling.

She heard the rumble of his laughter behind her, but she didn't turn to look again.

CHAPTER THREE

The Top-Secret Diary of Kyle O. Anderson

BOY, people are dumb, even Miss Maple, who up until yesterday I thought might be one of the smarter ones. She was waiting for me when I got to school. I got the big lecture about saying things that can be misinterpreted. Is it so hard to figure out a kid who protects a frog isn't likely to burn down the school?

Sheesh. I only said that because I had read it the night before in *The History of Khan*. Genghis Khan used to surround a city, and then he gave them the opportunity to surrender. If they didn't surrender he'd burn it to the ground, until the streets ran with fat melting from bodies. Is that the scariest thing you ever heard? That's where the expression "the wrath of Khan" comes from. Even Casper, who is really dumb, got it.

Miss Maple is dumb in a different way than Casper. Not just that she thought I might burn the school down when I couldn't even hurt a frog, but I saw the look on her face yesterday when she left my uncle. Not much room to misinterpret that. All pink and flustered.

And him talking about bubble baths. If you want to know what embarrassment feels like, try your uncle telling your teacher to have a bubble bath. I didn't miss the fact he's progressed to her first name, either.

Not that I thought about it, but if I had, I could have guessed her name would be something like Beth or Molly or Emily.

I was hoping the frog thing would warn her off us, but it kind of backfired.

She and Uncle Ben, the lady-killer, ended up at Migg's Pond together. Shoot. It's full of mud and mosquitoes, but they were talking away as if they were having a glass of wine over dinner at a five-star hotel.

I didn't know my uncle Ben came back here because of me and my Mom, though it could be a lie. I bet he knows exactly how to worm into the heart of someone as dumb as Miss Maple.

If they get together, I bet I'm out in a blink. Nobody wants a dorky eleven-year-old around when they're getting ready to make kissy-face. Ask me. I've been through it before. With Larry and Barry.

The frog was lame. Well, not totally lame because I still have him. He's not exactly a great pet, like a dog or a horse, but when I got to the pond, I couldn't let him go. The weather's getting colder and I'm not sure what frogs do when it gets cold. I don't want to think about him dying, that's for sure. Where would he go when he dies? I'm not sure about heaven. Even if there is one, I don't know if they let frogs in. I don't know if they'll let my Mom in, either. She never went to church, and she sure swore a lot and stuff.

Miss Maple has the stupidest car you ever saw. It's

like a hundred years old, a red VW convertible. She loves that car. You can tell by the way she keeps care of it, all shiny all the time, the way she drives it with her nose in the air.

I guess if I really need her to hate me, I could always do something to the car. It would be just too much to hope that I could make her think my uncle did it. Maybe I better wait and think about this. My uncle will probably take my frog away if I do something that bad to *Beth*. I don't know how somebody who has probably killed people with his bare hands deals with a frog, but whatever he does, I have a feeling it would be better than if Casper Hearn got his big fat mitts on it.

I hope I don't have to do anything to Miss Maple's car. That will be my last resort. And not because of Kermit. I'm not dumb enough to get attached to a frog.

I hope I don't have to make her hate me too bad.

This was looking good, Ben thought, looking at the call display on his cell phone. Miss Beth Maple was calling him again. Two calls in two days.

Though maybe yesterday didn't count, since his nephew had been missing. She was kind of obligated to call about something like that.

But even she couldn't have two emergencies in two days.

He hoped she was calling to tell him about the bubble bath. Though the thought of her telling him such a thing made him want to laugh out loud, because it would be so impossibly not her. Delightful, though, if you were the one she decided to let down her hair for.

Because there was definitely something about her, just beneath the surface. It was as if, as uptight as she seemed to be, she just hadn't had the right guy help her unlock her secrets. He thought of the line of her lips, wondered what it would be like to taste them, and then found he was the one to feel kind of flustered, like he was blushing, which was impossible. No one who spent eight years in the marines had anything like a blush left in them.

Unless what she had, innocence, was contagious.

And why did that make him feel oddly wistful, as if a man could ever be returned to what he had been before?

The truth was that Ben Anderson had had his fill of hard times and heartaches: his parents had died when he was young; he had lost his sister long before a doctor had told him she was going to die; he'd buried men he had shared a brotherhood with.

He could not ever be what he had been before. He could not get back the man who was unguarded, open to life. Long ago, he could remember being a young boy, Kyle's age, and every day ended with the words *"I love you"* to his mom and dad.

He could not be that again.

A memory, unbidden, came to him. His mother getting in the car, blowing him a kiss, and mouthing the words *"I love you"* because at seventeen he didn't want them broadcasted down the street.

Ben had not said those words since then, not ever. Was it insane to see them as a harbinger to disaster, to loss? He did not consider himself a superstitious man, but in this instance he was.

"Hello?" he said, aware that something cautious had entered his tone. He was not what she needed.

He was probably not what any woman needed. Damaged. Commitment-phobic.

"There were problems again today at school," she said wearily.

Considering he had just decided he was not what any woman needed, Ben was inordinately pleased that she had phoned to tell him about her problems! Nice. She probably had a little ache right between her shoulder blades, that he could—

"Kyle put glue on Casper's seat during recess. Not like the kind of glue we use at school for making fall leaves. I've never seen glue like that before."

Construction-site glue, Ben guessed, amazingly glum she wasn't phoning to share her problems with him. No, this was all about *his* problem.

"Casper stuck to the chair. And then he panicked and ripped the seat out of his pants when he tried to get out of the chair." There was a strangled sound from her end of the phone.

"Are you *laughing*?" he asked.

"No." It was a squeak.

"I think you are."

Silence, followed by a snort. And then another, muffled.

"Ah," he said. He could picture her, on the other end of the phone, holding back her laughter, trying desperately to play the role of the strict schoolmarm. He wished he was there to see the light in her eyes. He bet her nose crinkled when she laughed.

After a long time, struggling, she said, "There has to be a consequence. And he can never, *ever* guess I laughed."

"Oh," he teased, "a secret between us. This is even better than I could have hoped."

"If you could be mature, I thought we should talk about the consequence together," she said, her voice all grade-five schoolmistress again.

"I've always thought maturity was a good way to take all the fun out of life, but I will try, just for you."

"I hope you didn't suggest the glue to him!"

The truth was he might have, but his and Kyle's relationship had not progressed to sharing ideas for dealing with the class bully. He decided it was not in his best interest to share that with Miss Maple.

"We have to be on the same page." Sternly.

"Grown-ups against kids. Got it."

Silence. "I wasn't thinking of it that way. As if it's a war."

"A football game, then?"

"It's not really about winning and losing," she said carefully. "It's about finding what motivates Kyle. The class has a swim day coming up. I was going to suggest Kyle not be allowed to go. I hope that doesn't seem too harsh."

"No less than what he deserves. I'll let him know."

"Thank you." And then, hesitating, "You won't tell him—"

"That you laughed? No. I'll keep that to myself. Treasure it. It's something no grade-five boy needs to know about his teacher."

"Thank you for your cooperation," she said formally, and hung up the phone.

Ben went and found Kyle. He didn't have to look far. Kyle was in his room, the music booming. He was trying to get his frog to eat dead flies.

"Ah, Miss Maple just called. I heard about what you did to Casper."

"They can't prove it was me."

"Yeah, well, you're not going on the class swim trip that's coming up because of it."

"Boo-hoo," Kyle said, insincerely. Unless Ben was mistaken, rather than seeing his absence on the class trip as a punishment, Kyle was gleeful about it!

Unremorseful, Kyle went back to feeding his frog. Its long tongue snaked out, and the fly he had thrown in was grabbed from the air and disappeared.

"Wow," Kyle said. "Was that the coolest thing ever?"

Ben thought it was the first time he'd ever seen his nephew look truly happy. Silly to want to call Miss Maple back and tell her about it. Ridiculous to want to hear her laugh again.

If he wanted to hear laughter, he just had to turn on the television.

Except he didn't have one anymore. It was in Kyle's room. And besides, listening to a laugh track was going to seem strangely empty after hearing her trying to choke back her chortles.

"Wanna go for ice cream?" he asked Kyle. Too late, he realized he was letting down the home team. Since swimming had been no kind of consequence at all, he probably shouldn't be taking Kyle for ice cream. It was almost like saying, *Go ahead. Glue Casper to his seat. I think its funny.*

Which, come to think of it, he did.

"Ripped the whole seat out of his pants?" he asked Kyle as they walked down to Friendly's, the best ice cream store in Cranberry Corners.

"Yeah, and he had on blue underwear with cowboys on it."

"Oh, *baby* underwear."

And then he and his nephew were laughing, and despite the fact he was letting down the home team, Ben wouldn't have traded that moment for the whole wide world.

She phoned again the following night.

"I think he was very upset about the swimming being canceled," she confided in Ben. "Everybody else was talking about it all day, especially Casper. And he was left out."

Ben remembered Kyle's gleeful *boo-hoo*.

"He didn't even try to do the class assignment, but I'm remiss to punish him again so soon. Just to punish him will make him feel defeated," she told him. "You have to reward him when he does good things."

"Look, the only thing he does around here is feed his frog. I can't exactly reward him for that."

"I think rewarding him for being responsible for his pet would be good!"

Ben mulled that over. "Okay. I'm going to take him for ice cream." He hesitated. "Want to come?"

She hesitated, too. "I shouldn't."

"Why not? We're on the same team, right? I bet you like vanilla."

"That makes me sound dull."

"Surprise me, then."

And she did surprise him, for showing up at all, and for showing up on her bicycle with her hair down, surprisingly long, past her shoulders, her lovely cheeks pink from exertion.

"I didn't know teachers wore shorts," Kyle said, spotting her first. He frowned. "That should be against the law."

Ben agreed. Even though Beth's shorts would be considered very conservative, ending just above her knee, her legs could cause traffic accidents! They were absolutely gorgeous.

"What's she doing here?" Kyle asked as she came toward them.

"She's going to have ice cream with us."

"Oh," Kyle said, "you *invited* her." He did not sound pleased. He did not sound even a little bit pleased, but what eleven-year-old wanted to have ice cream with his teacher?

She wouldn't let Ben order for her or pay for her, but he watched closely all the same. When she joined them at a small table outside, she had ordered some hellish looking mix of orange and black.

"Tiger," she informed Ben. Then she went on to prove that she could more than surprise him. Who would have guessed that watching that prim little schoolmarm licking an ice cream cone could be the most excruciatingly sensual experience of a somewhat experienced guy's life? When a blob of the quickly melting brackish material fell on her naked thigh, he thought there wasn't enough ice cream in the world to cool down the heat inside of him.

He leaped to his feet, consulted his watch with an astounded frown. "Kyle and I have to go," he announced. "School night. That homework thing."

She should have looked pleased that he was being such a responsible guardian. She *would* have looked pleased to know he was going if she knew what he was thinking about her thighs. And ice cream. In the same sentence.

He'd annoyed her. Actually, he thought she was more

than annoyed. Mad. He didn't blame her. He'd invited her for ice cream and then ditched her. She might never know how noble his departure had been. It had been for the protection of both of them.

Kyle seemed mad at him, too. When Ben pressed him about his homework, Kyle said, as regally as a prince who did not toil with the peasants, "I don't do homework."

And instead of thinking of some clever consequence, to go with *the plan*, Ben said, "Well, fail grade five then. See if I care."

Ben Anderson wished his life could go back to being what it had been such a short while ago. Frozen dinners. Guy nights. A home gym in the spare bedroom.

And at the same time he wished it, he missed it when she didn't call him the next night, or the one after that, either. That either meant *the plan* was working, or she was giving up.

Or that his foolish mixing of her professional life with her personal one had left her nearly as confused as it had left him. He doubted he'd been forgiven for leaving her in the lurch with her tiger ice cream. Now she had probably vowed not to speak to Ben Anderson again unless Kyle turned her world upside down.

Should he phone her? And tell her he rewarded Kyle every night for feeding and caring for his frog, trying to make up for the fifth-grade-failure comment. But the reward was ice cream, and Ben didn't think it would be a very good idea to mention ice cream around her for a while.

Besides, after that shared moment of camaraderie over Casper's unfortunate choice of underwear, Kyle had retreated into a sullen silence.

After a week of trying out excuses in his head to phone her, and discarding each one as more lame than the last, the decision was taken out of Ben's hands.

The school's number came up on his cell phone's display. He knew it could be anyone. The principal, the nurse, Kyle himself. But he also knew it was telling him something important that he hoped it was Beth.

And then was reminded to be careful what he hoped for!

He had to hold the phone away—way away—from his ear. Kyle had been right about one thing. She did have kind of a screechy voice—when she was upset, and she was very upset.

She finally paused for breath, a hiccupping sound that made him wonder if she was crying. He did not want to think of Beth Maple crying.

"Let me get this straight," he said uneasily. "While you took the class swimming, somebody took a nail and scratched my company name in the side of your car? Are you kidding me?"

He didn't know why he said that because it was more than obvious she wasn't kidding. He groaned when she told him what else was scratched in there.

"It sucks to be you." And of course, Kyle had not been swimming.

"I'll be there as soon as I can," he said, and hung up the phone. It occurred to him it was totally inappropriate to be whistling. Totally inappropriate to feel happy that he was going to be seeing her again so soon.

She might be able to make eating ice cream look like something out of the Kama Sutra, but he had just been screeched at! He had already deduced he was not the kind of man who could give a woman like that one thing she needed.

Except she did need to be kissed. He could tell by the way she ate ice cream! And he had it on good authority he was very good at that.

But it was not the thought of kissing her that made him happy, because obviously kissing a woman like that would make his life rife with complications that it did not currently have.

As if an eleven-year-old boy armed with a nail was not enough of a complication for him at the moment.

What seemed to be causing the renegade happiness was the thought of the look on her face a long time ago when he had told her about swimming in the dark: a moment of unguarded wonder and yearning, before she had quickly masked whatever she was feeling.

He wanted to make her look like that again.

He supposed it was a guy thing. A challenge.

He reminded himself sternly that his big challenge right now was the person who was vandalizing people's cars.

It was a big deal. A terrible thing for Kyle to have done. A betrayal of the teacher who had been nothing but good to him.

But Ben Anderson still whistled all the way to the school.

Beth Maple's car was about the cutest thing he had ever seen, a perfectly refurbished 1964 Volkswagen Beetle convertible, finished in candy-apple red. The car was kind of like her—sweet and understated, with the surprise element of the candy-apple red, and the unexpected sexiness of a convertible top.

Unfortunately, the car was marred right now. On the driver's side door someone had scratched "THE GARDEN OF WEDDING," an unfortunate misspelling of the name of Ben's business. Like most confirmed bachelors, he did not like weddings. He had never noticed before how close to the word *wedding* that *weedin'* was.

He was startled and horrified that even being in the near vicinity of that word and Beth at the same time, he could picture her as a bride, gliding down an aisle in a sea of virginal white.

Was she a virgin?

He could feel his face getting red, so he frowned hard at the words scratched in the side of her car. What the hell was going on with him? His self-control was legendary, and yet here were these renegade thoughts, just exploding in his mind without warning, as though he had stepped on a land mine. First the naughty thoughts around ice cream and now this.

"There's more," she said.

Yeah, there was, because as hard as he was trying to crowd out the picture of her in a wedding dress from his mind, not to mention that terrible none-of-your-business question, once you had allowed your mind to go somewhere like that, it was very hard to corral the wayward thoughts.

He slid a glance at her face, her smooth forehead marred by a frown, distress in her eyes, as if this was the very worst thing that had ever happened to her.

He would guess she *had* lived a sheltered life.

He followed her around to the passenger side, looked where she pointed. In smaller letters, lower case, was scratched deep into that candy-apple red paint "it sucks to be you."

As if Kyle wasn't the prime suspect anyway, he might as well have signed his handiwork with his own name.

Ben glanced at Beth Maple again. The teacher was looking distressed and pale, as if she was hanging on by a thread and the slightest thing would make her burst into tears.

Which was something Ben Anderson did not want to see at all. The wedding thoughts and *the* question were about as much stress as he wanted for one day. A woman like that, in tears, could be his undoing. It could make a man feel all big and strong and protective. He didn't want to feel like that. He was as unsuited to the role of riding in on his charger to rescue the damsel in distress as he was to the role of standing at the top of that aisle, waiting…

And reacting to tears moved a man toward emotional involvement, and as challenging as he found the prim schoolteacher, he wanted to play with her, that delicious wonderful exhilarating man/woman game where you parted with a kiss and no hard feelings when it was all over.

He did not want to play the game that ended with white dresses, no matter how lovely that vision might be.

He slid a look at her and wondered when he had become so imaginative. Today she was wearing a white sweater and a black skirt and a lavender blouse with lace on it.

Not an outfit that should make a man think of weddings or virginity. Or of bubble baths or swimming in dark ocean waters. At all.

But that is where his unruly male mind went nonetheless.

Her hair was still wet from the class trip, and he wondered what she had worn at the pool. A one-piece, he decided. Matching shorts, that she probably hadn't taken off. Not what she would wear for a midnight swim with him.

He had the sudden, disturbing thought that it might not be exactly ethical to play with Miss Maple. She wasn't the kind of woman who understood the rules he played by. The thought was disturbing because he did not think thoughts like that. She was an adult. He was an adult. Couldn't they just dance around each other a bit and see where it went?

No. It was a whisper. His conscience? Or maybe his bachelor survival instincts. Beware of women who make you think of weddings.

Funny, that of all the women he had gone out with, she, the least threatening, and certainly the least sexy, would be the one who would make him feel as if he needed to be the most wary, the most on guard. Because she had a sneaky kind of sexiness that crept up on you, instead of the kind that hit you over the head.

He slid her another look. No. Not the least sexy. Not at all. No, that wasn't quite it. She wasn't *overtly* sexy. Sneaky sexy in this kind of understated virginal way that could set his blood on fire. If he let it. Which he wasn't going to. He had set his formidable will and sense of discipline against greater obstacles than her.

He turned his focus to his nephew, a welcome diversion, even in these uncomfortable circumstances.

Kyle was also standing off to the side of the car, looking into the distance, as if all this kafuffle had nothing to do with him. He looked pale to Ben, his freckles standing out against the white of his skin. He met his uncle's accusing gaze with nothing even resembling remorse.

But it wasn't quite belligerence, either. Amazingly it reminded Ben of the look on young soldiers' faces when they were scared to death to do something but did what they had to do anyway.

There was a weird kind of bravery in what Kyle had done.

Between her near tears and Kyle's attitude, Ben's happiness was dissipating more rapidly than a snowball in August.

"I *love* this car," Beth said sadly.

And Ben could tell it was true. He could tell by the sparkle shine on the wax, and the buffed white of the convertible top. He could tell by the way her fingers trembled on the scratch marks that she had been hurt and deeply.

A man allergic to love, he should have *approved* of her affection for the car. Why did it seem like a waste to him? Why would a woman like that waste her love on what really was just a hunk of metal and moving parts?

Because it was safe. It was a startling and totally unwanted insight into her. He slid her a look. Ah, yes, he should have seen it before.

The kind of woman who could be least trusted with the kind of man he was. He liked things light and lively and superficial, and he could see, in this moment of vulnerability, that she had already been scarred by someone. Heartbroken. Bruised.

Along with the uncontrolled direction of his own thoughts, it was a back-off insight if he had ever had one. But instead of wanting to back off, he felt a strange desire to fix it. He felt even more like he wanted to see that look on her face again that he had seen when he had told her about swimming in the dark, a look of yearning, of wonder.

"I don't understand," Beth said to Kyle, struggling for composure. "Why would you do this to me? I've been good to you, haven't I?"

Kyle didn't look at her. "What makes you think I did it?" he tried for uncaring, but his voice wavered. "Are you going to get DNA from a scratch mark? It could have been Casper Hearn. He hates me. He would try and make it look like me."

Beth had the bad judgment to look doubtful.

But Ben knew now was the wrong time to let his bewilderment at Kyle's strange bravery, or sympathy for Kyle's past, in any way temper his reaction to this. It was vandalism, and no matter what had motivated it, it couldn't be tolerated or let go. It would be so much easier to let it go, to excuse it in some way, so that he didn't have to tangle any further with a woman who made him think renegade thoughts of weddings and virginity.

But he couldn't. This kid had been entrusted to him, and now he had to do the right thing. Every single time. They had tried Beth's *plan*, her way, but they didn't have time to fool with this any longer, to experiment with the plan that would work for Kyle.

The damage to Beth's car was a terrible movement in the wrong direction for Kyle. If Ben let this slide, how long until the downward spiral of anger and bitterness could not be stopped? It seemed to him he had been here before, watched helplessly and from a distance, as a young person, Carly, had been lost to the swirling vortex of her own negative emotion.

"Kyle," he said sternly. "Stop it. I know it was you."

Beth looked as if she might be going to protest that they didn't have any proof, but Ben silenced her with a faintly lifted finger.

"I don't know why you did it," he continued, "and I don't want to hear excuses for the inexcusable. I do know Miss Maple didn't deserve it. And neither did I. Man up."

Something about those words *man up* hit Kyle. Ben could see them register in his eyes. He was being asked to be more, instead of less. Everything was going to be so much harder if Kyle made the wrong decision right now.

But he didn't. After a brief struggle, he turned to his teacher. He said quietly, "I'm sorry." The quaver in his voice worsened.

"But why?" she asked, and her voice was quavering, too.

Kyle shrugged, toed the ground with his sneaker, glanced at his uncle with a look so transparent and beseeching Ben thought his heart would break.

Care about me, anyway. Please.

And Ben planned to. But he was so aware of the minefield he was trying to cross.

The wrong kind of caring at this turning point in Kyle's life could destroy him.

Funny. Ben was allergic to that word *love*. He *never* used it. And yet when he looked at his nephew, troubled, so very young, so needy, he knew that's what he felt for him.

And that he could not express it any longer in a way that might be misconstrued as weakness. Kyle needed leadership right now. Strong leadership. Implacable.

Ben folded his arms over his chest and gave his nephew his most steely-eyed look.

"You made this mess," he said quietly. "You're going to have to fix it."

"I don't know how," Kyle said.

"Well, I do. There's probably close to a thousand bucks worth of damage there. Do you have a thousand dollars?"

"I don't have any money," Kyle said. "I didn't even get allowance last week, cuz I didn't take out the garbage."

"Do you have anything worth a thousand dollars?"

"No," Kyle whispered.

This was part of the problem. His nephew was the kid who perceived he had nothing of value. And he probably didn't have the things the other kids in his class had and took for granted. There had been no fifty-inch TV sets, no designer labels. Ben had bought him a nice bicycle once, and as far as he could tell it had disappeared into the dark folds of that shadowy world his sister lived in before Kyle had ever even ridden it.

"I guess she'll have to call the insurance company, then," Ben said. "They'll want a police report filed."

Beth and Kyle both gasped.

"Unless you can come up with something you have of value."

Kyle's shoulders hunched deeper as he considered a life bereft of value. Beth was looking daggers at Ben.

Didn't she get it? He deserved to be afraid. He *needed* to be afraid. Ben watched, letting the boy flounder in his own misery. He let him nearly drown in it, before he tossed him the life rope.

"Maybe you have something of value," he said slowly.

"I do?"

"You have the ability to sweat, and maybe we can talk Miss Maple into trading some landscaping for what you owe her. But she'll have to agree, and you'll have to do the work. What do you say, Miss Maple?"

"Oh," she breathed, stunned, and then the look of wonder was there, just for a fraction of a second. "Oh, you have no idea. My yard is such a mess. I bought the house last year, after—" She stopped abruptly, but Ben knew. The house was the same as the car. *Safe.* Purchased to fill a life and to take the edge off a heartbreak.

He could see that as clearly in the shadows of her eyes as if she had spoken it out loud.

Move away, marine. But he didn't.

"And you're willing to do the work, Kyle?"

Kyle still seemed to be dazed by the fact he had something of value. "Yeah," he said quickly, and then, in case his quick reply might be mistaken for enthusiasm, shrugged and added, "I guess."

"No guessing," Ben said. "Yes or no."

"Yes."

"Good man."

And as hard as he tried not to show it, Kyle could not hide the fact that small compliment pleased him.

An hour later they pulled up in front of Miss Beth Maple's house. Even if the tiny red car had not been parked in the driveway, Ben would have known it was her house, and his suspicions around her ownership would have been confirmed. It was like a little cottage out of *Snow White,* an antidote for a heartache if he'd ever seen one.

It was the kind of place a woman bought when she'd decided to go it on her own, when she had decided she was creating her own space, and it was going to be safe and cozy, an impregnable female bastion of good taste and white furniture and breakable bric-a-brac.

"It looks like a dollhouse," Kyle said, with male uneasiness that Ben approved of.

It was a tidy house, painted a pale-buttercup yellow, the gingerbread and trim around the windows painted deep midnight blue. Lace curtains blew, white and virginal as a damned wedding dress, out a bedroom window that was open to the September breezes.

It was a reminder, Ben thought, getting out of the truck, that she was not the kind of woman a man could play with, have a casual good time for a couple of weeks or a couple of months and then say goodbye with no hurt feelings on either side.

No, the house spoke of a woman who wanted things, and was afraid of the very things she wanted. Stability. A safe haven. A world that she could trust.

Ben wanted to just drive away from all the things she would be shocked he could see in that neat facade. But he had to do the responsible thing now, for his nephew.

The yard was as neglected as the house was tidy. Yellow climbing roses had gone wild over the arbor over the front gate, and it was nearly falling down under their weight. Inside the yard, the grass was cut, but dead in places, a shrub under the front window had gotten too big and blocked out the front of the house and probably the light to the front room.

Beth Maple came out her door. Ben tried not to stare.

She had gotten home before they had arrived, and she'd had time to change. She was barefoot, and had on a pair of canvas pants, rolled to the knee, with a drawstring waist. Somehow the casual slacks were every bit as sexy as the shorts she had worn the night she had joined them for ice cream, though he was not sure how that was possible, since the delicate lines of her legs were covered.

Imagination was a powerful thing. The casual T-shirt just barely covered her tummy. If he made her stretch up, say to show him those roses, he could catch a glimpse of her belly button.

What would the point of that be, since he had decided he was not playing the game with her? That he was going to try and fix something for her, not make it worse! Seeing her house had only cemented that decision.

"It's awful, I know," she said ruefully, looking at the yard. "I only bought the place a year ago. I'm afraid there was so much to do inside. Floors refinished, windows reglazed, some plumbing problems." Her voice drifted away in embarrassment.

Ben saw she had an expectation of perfection for herself. She didn't like him seeing a part of her world that was not totally under control.

"I don't imagine a thousand dollars will go very far," she said.

But Ben was going to make it go as far as it needed to go to wear Kyle out, to make him understand the value of a thousand dollars, and the price that had to be paid when you messed with someone else's stuff.

And working at Miss Maple's would be a relatively small price compared to what it could have been if she called the cops.

"You might be surprised how far your thousand dollars will go," he said, and watched as Kyle fixated on the large side yard's nicest feature, a huge mature sugar maple just starting to turn color. It reminded Ben of the tree in her classroom.

His nephew scrambled up the trunk and into the branches. Ben was relieved to see him do such a simple, ordinary, boy thing.

Beth watched Kyle for a moment, too, something in her eyes that Ben tried to interpret and could not, and then turned back to him.

"What should we fix?" she said briskly. "The arbor? The railing up the front stairs? The grass?"

Suddenly Ben did interpret the look in her eyes. It was wistfulness. She wanted to climb that tree! To be impulsive and free, hidden by the leaves, scrambling higher, looking down on the world from a secret perch. Was her affection for the tree the reason she had reproduced it in her classroom? Was she even aware of her own yearnings?

"How do you want this yard to make you feel?" he asked.

"Wow. You can make me feel something for a thousand dollars?"

For some reason his eyes skidded to her lips. He could make her feel something for free. But he wasn't going to.

"I can try," he said gruffly.

"Okay," she said, challenging, as if he'd asked for more than he had bargained for, "I want that summer day feeling. A good book. A hammock in the shade. An ice-cold glass of lemonade. I want to feel lazy and relaxed and like I don't have to do a lick of work."

Low maintenance. He began a list in his head. But when he thought of low maintenance, he wasn't really thinking about her yard. He was thinking about her. He bet she would be one of those low-maintenance girls. She wouldn't need expensive gifts or jewelry or tickets to the best show in town to make her happy.

A picnic blanket. A basket with fried chicken. A bottle of something sparkly, not necessarily wine.

Why did Beth Maple do this to him? Conjure up pictures of things he would be just as happy not thinking about?

Still what people wanted in their yards told him a great deal about them. It was possible that she just didn't know what was available, what was current in outdoor living spaces.

"You know," he said carefully, "lots of people now are making the yard their entertainment area. Outdoor spaces are being converted into outdoor rooms: kitchens with sinks and fridges, BBQ's and bars. Hardscaping is my specialty. Last week I did an outdoor fireplace, copper-faced, and patio where you could easily entertain forty or fifty people."

"Hardscaping?" she said. "I've never heard that term."

"It means all the permanent parts of the yard, so walkways and patios, canopies, privacy fences or enclosures, ponds. Basically anything that's made out of wood, concrete, brick or stone. I have other people do the greenscaping and the styling."

"Styling?"

"You know. Weather-resistant furniture. Outdoor carpeting."

"Obviously that isn't on a thousand-dollar budget."

"If there was no budget, what would you do?" he asked, having failed to find out how she felt about the posh entertainment area in her backyard.

She snorted. "Why even go there?"

"Landscaping doesn't have to be done all at once. I like to give people a master plan, and then they can do it in sections. Each bit of work puts a building block in place for the next part of the plan. A good yard can take five years to make happen." He smiled, "And a really good yard is a lifetime project."

She folded her arms over her chest. "The plan for a yard, alone, is probably worth more than what Kyle owes me."

"Well, if you don't tell him, I won't. He has nothing to give you right now, except his ability to work. If I take that away from him he has nothing at all."

She nodded, a kind of surrender. Definitely an agreement.

"I want him to have blisters on his hands, and that little ache between his shoulder blades from working in this yard."

"I'm not accepting charity from you," she said, stubbornly.

"And I'm not offering any. You wanted a plan for my nephew, and yours, so far, doesn't seem to be working that well. Now it's my turn. There has to be a price to be paid for what he did to your car, and it has to be substantial. No more rewards for feeding his frog."

"How long are you going to make him work for me?"

"Hopefully until he's eighteen," Ben said dryly. "So, tell me how you'd like to spend time in your yard."

"To be truthful the whole entertainment thing, like an outdoor kitchen and fireplace isn't really me. I mean, it sounds lovely, I'm sure you make wonderful yards for people, but I really do love the idea of simple things out here. A hammock. Lemonade. Book. I'd want a place that felt peaceful. Where you could curl up with a good book on a hot afternoon and listen to water running and birds singing, and glance up every now and then to see butterflies."

It wasn't fair, really. People did not know how easy it was to see their souls. Did he need to know this about her?

That in a world gone wild with bigger and better and more, in a world where materialism was everything, she somehow wanted the things money could not buy.

The miracle of butterfly wings, the song of birds, the sound of water.

She wanted a quiet place.

He imagined her bare feet in lush grass and was nearly blinded with a sense of desire. He was getting sicker by the minute. Now she didn't even need to be eating ice cream for him to be entertaining evil male thoughts.

He saw her gaze move to Kyle in the tree again, wistful, and suddenly he was struck by what he wanted to do for her.

"What would you think about a tree house?" he said softly. And saw it. A flash of that look he had glimpsed twice, and now longed for. Wonder. Hope. Curiosity.

"A tree house?" she breathed. "Really?"

"Not a kid's tree house," he said, finding it taking shape in his mind as he looked at the tree, "an adult retreat. I could build a staircase that wound around the trunk of that tree, onto a platform in the branches. We could put a hammock up there and a table to hold the lemonade."

He thought he would build her a place where the birds could sing sweetly, so close she could touch them. He would put a container garden up there, full of the flowers that attracted butterflies. Below the tree, a simple water feature. She could stand at the rail and look down on it; she would be able to hear the water from her hammock.

"That sounds like way too much," she said, but her protest was weak, overridden by the wonder in her eyes as she gazed at that tree, beginning to see the possibility.

To see her at school, prim and tidy, a person would never guess how her eyes would light up at the thought of her own tree house. But Ben had always known, from the first moment, that she had a secret side to her. The tree in her classroom had held the seeds of this moment.

He was not sure it was wise to uncover it. And he was also not sure if he could stop himself, which was an amazing thought in itself since he considered self-discipline one of his stronger traits.

"We'll take it one step at a time." That way he could back off if he needed to. But then he heard himself committing to a little more, knowing he could not leave this project until he saw the light in her eyes reach full fruition. He did a rough calculation in his head. "We'll come every day for two weeks after school. We'll see if he's learned what he needs to learn by then."

She turned her attention from the tree and he found himself under the gaze of those amazing eyes. He knew, suddenly, he was not the only one who saw things that others did not see.

"There are a lot of ways to be a teacher, aren't there, Ben?"

She said it softly, as if she admired something about him. In anyone else, that would be the flirt, the invitation to start playing the game with a little more intensity, to pick up the tempo.

But from her it was a compliment, straight from her heart. And it went like an arrow to his, and penetrated something he had thought was totally protected in armor.

"Thanks," he said, softly. "We'll be here tomorrow, right after school." He turned and called his nephew.

They watched as he scrambled out of the tree.

"We're going to come, starting tomorrow after school," Ben told him. "We're going to build Miss Maple a tree house."

Kyle's eyes went round. "A tree house?" For the first time since they had laughed together about Casper's underwear, his defensive shield came down. "Awesome," he breathed.

"Awesome," she agreed.

Kyle actually smiled. A real smile. So genuine, and so revealing about who Kyle really was that it nearly hurt Ben's eyes. But then Kyle caught himself and frowned, as if he realized he had revealed way too much about himself.

Ben turned to go, thinking maybe way too much had been revealed about everybody today.

There are lots of ways to be a teacher. As if she saw in him the man he could be, as if she saw the heart that he had kept invisible, unreachable, untouchable, behind its armor. He could teach her a thing or two, too. But he wasn't going to.

CHAPTER FOUR

BETH Maple stood at her kitchen counter and listened to the steady thump of hammers in her yard. She contemplated how it was that her neatly structured life had been wrested so totally from her control.

"Uncle Ben, haven't you ever heard of skin cancer, for cripe's sake? The three *S*s? Slam on a hat, slather on sunscreen and slip on a shirt."

For a moment it only registered how sweet it was that Kyle was so concerned about his uncle.

But then she froze. *Ben Anderson had taken off his shirt? In her backyard?*

"I'll live dangerously," Ben called to his nephew.

Now *there* was a surprise, she thought dryly. *Don't peek,* she told herself, but that was part of having things wrested out of her control. Despite the sternness of the order she had given herself, she peeked anyway.

It was a gorgeous day. September sunshine filtering through yellow-edged leaves with surprising heat and bathing her yard in gold. Her yard actually looked worse than it had a few days ago, with spray-painted lines on her patches of grass, heaps of dirt, sawed-off branches and construction materials stacked up.

But the pure potential shone through the mess and made her feel not just happy but elated. Maybe when a person gave up a bit of control, it left room for life to bring in some surprises, like the one that was unfolding in her yard.

Of course, there was one place she had to keep her control absolute, and where she was failing, the order not to peek being a prime example. She had peeked anyway, and she felt a forbidden little thrill at what she was seeing.

Was it possible that sense of elation that filled her over the past few days had little to do with the yard?

Certainly the forbidden thrill had nothing to do with the landscaping progress in her yard.

No, there was enough heat in that afternoon sun that Ben Anderson had removed his shirt.

It was delicious to spy on him from the safety of her kitchen window, to look her fill, though she was not sure a woman could ever see enough of a sight like Ben Anderson, undressed.

He looked like a poster boy for *sexy,* all lean, hard muscle, taut, flawless skin, a smudge of dirt across the ridged plane of his belly, sweat shining in the deep hollow of his throat, just above the deep, strong expanse of a smooth chest. His jeans, nearly white with age and washing, hung low on the jut of his hips. His stomach was so flat that the jeans were suspended from hip to hip, creating a lip-licking little gap where the waistband was not even touching his skin.

Beth watched his easy swing of the hammer, the corresponding ripple of muscle. It made her feel almost dizzy. She had known from the start Ben Anderson needed a label. *Contents too potent to handle.* She had never gotten a thrill like this over the Internet, that was for sure!

It was embarrassing to be this enamored with his physical being, but he was so *real*. No wonder she had found her Internet romance as delightful as she had. The presence of a real man was anything but; it was disturbing.

It was disturbing to feel so tense around another human being, so aware of them, and so aware of unexplored parts of yourself.

Beth felt she would have been quite content to go through life without knowing that she possessed this *hunger*.

Now that she did know she possessed it, how did she go back to what she had been before? What did she do about it? Surrender? Fight it?

Surely baking cookies was no kind of answer! But it bought her time. Which she should have used wisely. She could have done an Internet search for *defenses against diabolically attractive men* instead of spying from her kitchen window!

This was the third time Ben and Kyle had been here, twice after school, short sessions where his shirt had stayed on. Though for Beth, seeing him deal with that fragile boy with just the right mix of sternness and affection had been attractive in and of itself. She could see that her initial assessment of Ben Anderson—that he could not be domesticated—had been inaccurate. When she saw his patience with Kyle, and the way he guided the child toward making his own decisions, she knew she was looking at a man who would be a wonderful daddy someday, who was growing in confidence in this role of mentor and guardian.

Now it was Saturday and Ben had shown up this morning, way too early, announcing they would spend the whole day.

Saturday was her sleep-in day, and her grocery day, and her laundry day, and her errand day, and she had canceled everything she normally would have done without a second thought. Groceries or hanging out with Ben Anderson. *Duh.*

The buzzer on the oven rang, and Beth moved, reluctantly, from the window and removed the cookies, dripping with melted chocolate chips, from her oven. While she waited for them to cool, she debated, milk or lemonade? Milk would go better with the cookies, lemonade would go better with the day.

That's what having a man like that in your yard did to you. Every decision suddenly seemed momentous. It felt as if her choice would say something about her. To him.

In the end she put milk and lemonade on the tray. To confuse him, just in case her choices were telling him anything about her.

He set down his hammer when he saw her coming, smiled that lazy, sexy smile that was setting her world on edge. Kyle, who was hard at work digging something, set down the shovel eagerly.

She had known Ben was a man with good instincts. This project was not just good for Kyle. The turnaround in his attitude seemed nothing short of spectacular. It was as if he had been uncertain he had any value in the world, and suddenly he saw what hard work—his hard work—could accomplish. He could see how the face of the world could be changed by him in small ways, like her yard. And the possibility of changing the world in big ways opened to him for the first time.

When Ben had unfolded his drawing of the yard, he had included his nephew and consulted with him, listened to him, showed respect for his opinions. And Ben had done the same for her.

The three of them were building something together, and in her most clear moments she was aware it was not just a tree house.

The plan that Ben had drawn for her tree retreat filled some part of her that she did not know had been empty. It was deceptively simple. A staircase spiraled around the tree trunk, though it actually never touched it, because Ben had been concerned about keeping the tree healthy, by not driving nails into the trunk or branches.

The staircase led to a simple railed platform that sat solidly in amongst the strongest branches, but was again supported mostly by the subtle use of posts and beams.

Ben's concern for the health of her tree had surprised her, showed her, again, that there was something more there than rugged appeal and rippling muscle. Ben had a thoughtfulness about him, though if she were to point it out, she was certain he would laugh and deny it.

She soon found out executing such a vision was not that simple. There had been digging, digging and more digging. Then leveling and compacting. She had insisted on having a turn on the compactor, a machine that looked like a lawn mower, only it was heavier and had a mind of its own.

Ben had turned it on, and while under his watchful eye she had tried to guide it around the base of the tree where there would be a concrete pad. The compactor was like handling a jackhammer. The shaking went up her whole body. She felt like a bobble-head doll being hijacked!

"Whoa," she called over and over, but the machine did not listen. Despite all Ben's efforts to be kind to the tree, she banged into the trunk of it three times.

Kyle finally yelled over the noise, begging her to stop, he was laughing so hard. And then she had dared to glance away from her work. Ben was laughing, too.

And then she was laughing, which the unruly machine took advantage of by taking off across her lawn and ripping out a patch of it, until Ben grabbed it and shut it off and gently put her away from it.

"Miss Maple?"

"Yes?"

"You're fired."

When had she last laughed like that? Until her sides hurt? Until everything bad that had ever happened to her was washed away in the golden light of that shared moment? The laughter had made her feel new and alive, and as though life held possibilities that she had never dreamed of.

Possibilities as good as or even better than the tree sanctuary that was becoming a reality in her backyard.

The world she had allowed herself to have suddenly seemed way too rigid, the dreams she had given up on beckoned again. Everything *shimmered*, but was it an illusion of an oasis or was it something real?

Watching Ben work made it harder to see those distinctions, flustered her, and made her feel off balance. When a concrete truck had arrived, she had watched as Ben, so sure of himself, so in charge, so at ease, had directed that spout of creamy cement, pouring concrete footings, a pad for the staircase and a small patio.

It was his world. He was in charge. Competent. Decisive. All business and no nonsense as he showed Kyle what needed to be done. The concrete work seemed so hard, and yet there was nothing in him that shirked from it, he seemed to *enjoy* using his strength to create such lasting structures. That alone was deeply attractive in ways she didn't quite understand, but it was when the concrete was beginning to set that he added the *shimmer*.

The stern expression of absolute concentration fell away. He set down the trowel he'd been using and showing Kyle how to use. "Come on over, Beth, let's show them forever who did this."

Not a man you wanted to use your name in the same sentence that contained the word *forever*. Even if you did dream such things.

And he bent over and put his hands in the setting concrete.

And then he insisted she leave her prints there beside his. Kyle added his handprints happily, writing his name under his handprint, giving her a sideways look.

"Can I write, *it sucks to be you*?"

And then they had all laughed. *Again*. That beautiful from-the-belly laughter that felt as if it had the power to heal everything that was wrong in the world. Her world, anyway.

"Did you know," Ben asked her solemnly, "that your nose crinkles when you laugh?"

She instinctively covered her nose, but he pulled her concrete-covered hand away.

"You don't want to get that stuff on your face," he said, and then added, "It's cute when your nose does that."

She had been blissfully unaware until very recently that there was anything in her world that was wrong, that needed to be healed.

Beth had been convinced she was over all that nonsense with Rock/Ralph. Completely.

But now, as her world got bigger and freshened with new experiences and with laughter, and with a man who noticed her nose crinkled when she laughed and thought it was cute, she saw how her hurt had made her world small. Safe, but small.

Now it was as if something magic was unfolding in her yard, and the three of them were helpless against its enchantment. She had actually considered having Kyle put those words in there, *it sucks to be you*, because with those words this funny, unexpected miracle had been brought to her.

Not just the tree house.

Maybe the tree house was even the least of it. This *feeling* of working toward a common goal with other people, of being part of something. This *feeling* of the tiniest things, like washing the concrete off their hands with the hose, Ben reaching over and scrubbing a spec of stubborn grit off her hand, being washed in light, the ordinary becoming extraordinary.

Who was she kidding? The feeling was of belonging. The feeling was of excitement. It was as if something was unfolding just below the surface, as if the excitement in her life had just begun. As that the yard took shape, her staircase beginning to wind around the tree, it was as if she saw possibility in a brand-new way.

Now, as she came out the door with her tray of goodies and set them on the worn picnic table that once had been the pathetic centerpiece of her yard, she watched Ben stop what he was doing. He walked toward her, scooping up his T-shirt as he came, giving his face and chest a casual swipe with it, before pulling it over that incredible expanse of naked male beauty.

"Milk and lemonade," he said, grinning, eyeing the contents of the tray. "Interesting."

"Why?" she demanded. She had just known he would read something into whatever choice she made! She should have known not making a choice had a meaning, too.

He laughed. "You're trying to make everybody happy."

"No," she said, and put the tray down, stood with her hands on her hips staring at the reality of the staircase starting to gracefully curve around the tree, "you are. And look at my yard." But she wanted to say *Look at me. Can't you tell how happy I am?* Instead she said, "Look at Kyle."

Kyle arrived at the picnic table, smudges of dirt on his face, glowing with something suspiciously like happiness even without the choice between lemonade and milk.

"Look," he crowed, and showed her his hand.

A blister was red across the palm.

"Oh," she said, "that's terrible. I'll get some ointment."

But his uncle nudged her and shook his head. "It's part of being a man," he said.

Just loud enough for Kyle to hear him.

Kyle's chest filled with air, and he grinned happily, dug into the cookies and didn't look up until the plate was nearly emptied. He drank two glasses of milk and one of lemonade, and then leaped up and went back to what he'd been doing.

"Okay, I admit it," she said, watching the boy pick up his shovel. "Your plan is better than mine. He loves this. He is a different boy than he was a few days ago."

"Well, don't say it too loud or he might feel driven to prove you wrong, but, yeah, it's good for him."

"It's really good of you to do this. I'm sure today should have been your day off."

"I don't take much time off at this time of year. It gets slow when the weather changes, and then I take some time."

"And do what?" Was it too personal? Of course it was. She didn't want to know what he did with his spare time. *Yes, she did.*

"Usually I go back to Hawaii for a couple of weeks." His eyes drifted to Kyle. "This year, I'm not sure."

"How is your sister?" She could tell right away that *this* was too personal, by the way his shoulders stiffened, how he swirled lemonade in the bottom of his glass like a fortune-teller looking for an answer.

She could tell this was the part of himself that he didn't want people to know about. It was easy for him to be charming and fun-loving. She almost held her breath waiting to see what he would show her.

And then sighed with relief when he showed her what was real.

He rolled his big shoulders, looked away from the lemonade and held her gaze for one long, hard moment. "She's not going to make it."

Beth had known Kyle's mother was seriously ill. There was no other reason that Ben would have been appointed his guardian. But she was still taken aback at this piece of news.

She touched his arm. Nothing else. Just touched him. And it felt as if it was the most right thing in the world when his hand came and covered hers. Something connected them. Not sympathy, but something bigger, a culmination of something that had started happening in this yard from the first moment he had said he would build a tree house for her.

She could have stayed in that wordless place of connection for a long time. But his reaction was almost the opposite of hers.

He took his hand away as if he could snatch back the feeling that had just passed between them. He smiled at her, that devil-may-care smile, and she realized a smile, even a sexy one—or maybe especially a sexy one—could be a mask.

"I'm going to kiss you one day," he promised.

Was that a mask, too? A way of not feeling? Of not connecting on a *real* level? She looked at his lips.

The terrible truth was she was dying to be kissed by him.

But not like that. Not as part of a pretext, a diversion, a way to stop things from hurting.

"Actually, you're not," she said, and was pleased by his startled expression, as if no one had ever refused him a kiss before.

Probably no one had. And probably she was going to regret it tonight. Today. Seconds from now.

Before that weakness settled in, she got up and gathered up the tray and headed for the house. She pulled open the screen door with her toe and looked over her shoulder.

"You know," she called back to him, "kissing can't solve your problems. They will still be there after you unlock lips."

He sat there, looking as if a bomb had hit him, and then got up and stalked across the yard, stood at the bottom of her steps, glaring up at her.

"How would you know what kissing solves or doesn't solve?" he asked her darkly.

"What are you saying? That I look like I've never been kissed?"

"As a matter of fact, you don't look like any kind of an expert on the subject!"

That exquisite moment when she had felt so connected to him was gone. Completely. Absolutely. The oasis was an illusion, after all.

"You pompous, full-of-yourself Neanderthal," she sputtered.

"Don't call me names over five syllables."

"It was four! But just in case you didn't get it, it's the long version of caveman."

He looked like he was going to come up the stairs and tangle those strong, capable hands in her hair, and kiss her just to prove his point. Or hers. That he was a caveman.

But his point would be stronger; she would probably be such a helpless ninny under his gorgeous lips, just like a thousand helpless ninnies before her, that she would totally forget he was a caveman. Or forgive him for it. Or find it enchanting.

She slid inside the door, let it slap shut behind her and then turned, reached out with her little finger from under the tray and latched it.

"Did you just lock the door?" he asked, stunned.

She said nothing, just stood looking at him through the screen.

"What? Do you think I'd break down the door to kiss *you?*"

"It wouldn't be the first time," she said. Pique made her say it. Not that it was a complete lie. She had spent most of junior high hiding from the overly amorous affections of Harley Houston. Once he had leaped out of a coat closet at her, with his lips all puckered and ready. That was certainly close enough to breaking down a door.

Ben regarded her with ill-concealed temper. "It probably would."

"Look," she said coolly, "I don't understand, if you think I'm so incapable of inspiring great passion, why you're the one, who out of the blue, with no provocation *at all* on my part, said you would kiss me someday. As if it wasn't necessary for me to feel something first. Or you. As if you can just do that kind of thing because you feel like it and without the participation of the other person."

"Believe me, if I ever kissed you, you'd participate."

"I wouldn't," she said stubbornly, though she didn't want to be put to the test. And did want to be put to the test. Which most certainly meant she would fail any kind of participation test that involved his lips. Still, there was no sense feeding his already oversize ego. He was impossible. And aggravating. Irritating.

She had known he would be from the first time he had come into her classroom. And instead of letting good sense reign, what had she done?

She had been swayed by the most superficial of things. By his enormous good looks and by his even greater charm. By the sound of laughter. By a tree house taking shape in her yard.

She, Beth Maple, who really should have had so much more sense, had allowed their lives to tangle together! Given him her address, for God's sake. Allowed him into her yard. Baked him cookies. Fed him milk and lemonade.

She had shamelessly watched him take off his shirt and allowed him to put his big mitt prints in her concrete! Which would be a constant and irritating reminder of the fact that, given a chance, she could make a greater fool of herself for this man than she had for Rock aka Ralph!

She closed the inside door firmly, and locked it with as much noise as she could manage, too. But it wasn't until she was slamming dishes into the dishwasher that she realized he had gotten exactly what he wanted, after all, and it had never really been about a kiss.

He had been feeling something when he had told her his sister was going to die.

Sadness. Vulnerability. Maybe even trust in Beth.

And whether with a kiss or by starting an argument, he had managed to distance himself from his discomfort, move on.

No sense feeling a little soft spot for him because of that. It was a warning. There was no future with a man who was so shut off from his emotional self, who was so frightened of it.

When exactly had some sneaky little part of herself started contemplating some kind of future with *that* man?

"Never," she told herself later, as she watched him load up his tools and his nephew and drive away without saying goodbye, without even glancing at her windows. "I hope he never comes back," she told herself.

But when she wandered out in the yard and saw that the framework for the staircase was nearly completed, she knew he was coming back. If he was a quitter, he would have left right after the argument, and he hadn't.

The argument. She'd had her first argument with Ben Anderson.

And as silly as it seemed, she knew that real people disagreed. They had arguments. It was not like her relationship with Rock, which had unfolded like the fantasy it had turned out to be. Full of love notes and tender promises, not a cross word or a disagreement, only the gentlest of chiding on her part when Rock had been compelled to cancel yet one more rendezvous with his myriad of creative excuses.

"I'm probably not ready for real," she decided out loud, peering up through the thick leaves to where the platform would be.

But it was like being ready to be kissed by him. He didn't care if she was ready. If she wasn't very careful, he was just going to take her by storm whether she was ready or not.

And just like a storm, her life would be left in a wreckage after he was done blowing through. That's why storms of consequence had names. Hurricane Ben. Batten the hatches or evacuate?

"You're overreacting," she scolded herself. But she bet a lot of people said that when there was a storm brewing on the horizon.

To their peril.

CHAPTER FIVE

The Top Secret Diary of Kyle O. Anderson

I THINK Miss Maple and Uncle Ben had a fight. After she brought us out cookies and drinks—lemonade and milk—she went in the house and didn't come back out. My uncle didn't say goodbye to her when we left. He was pretty quiet on the drive home, but when I asked him if anything was wrong, he looked surprised and said, no everything was great, and how did I enjoy work today.

The truth? I really like working with my uncle. I love Miss Maple's tree house. I never, ever thought about the future before. I'm not one of those kids who always dreamed about being a fireman when I grew up.

Getting through each day seemed like a big enough undertaking to me.

But working with my uncle made me realize I like building things. And he says I'm good at it, too. When I suggested a way to change the steps so that they would work better, he said I was a genius. And one thing about my uncle, you can trust that when he says something like that, he means it.

If he did have a fight with Miss Maple, I'm really glad he didn't tell me about it. My mom always told me everything that was going on in her life, and if you think it feels good knowing all about grown-up problems, think again. Still, it's kind of funny, because I thought I wanted Uncle Ben and Miss Maple not to get along, but now that they aren't I feel worried about that.

When we got home, the phone was ringing and my uncle picked it up and gave it to me. The only person I could think of who would call me is my mom, so I nearly dropped the phone when it was Mary Kay Narsunchuk. She said that the planetarium was having a special show called Constellation Prize and would I like to go with her?

At first I thought it was a joke, like if I listened hard enough I would hear her girlfriends laughing in the background, but I didn't hear a sound.

"Why are you asking me?" I said, trying to sound cool and not too suspicious.

"Because you are the smartest person I know," she said, and I liked her saying that, even though we don't really *know* each other. And then she said she liked it that I protected the frog against Casper, even though she doesn't really like frogs.

She told me she hates Casper, which means we have something in common already.

Her mom picked me up at Uncle Ben's house and drove us to the planetarium, which was kind of dorky. I've been taking public transit by myself since I was six, and I don't really think the planetarium is in a rough neighborhood, so I thought the warnings to stand right outside the door when she came back to pick us up were hilarious, though I didn't laugh, just said yes, ma'am.

On the way in, I noticed Mary Kay is at least three inches taller than me, and had on really nice clothes, and that bad feeling started, like I'm not good enough. Then I told myself it wasn't like it was a date or anything, and when she asked what I had done today I told her about building the tree house for Miss Maple, and she thought that was the coolest thing she had ever heard.

The weirdest thing happened when we took our seats. The lights went out and she took my hand.

That was all. But the stars came on in the pitch-blackness, like lighted diamonds piercing black velvet, and I thought, *All of this is because of Kermit*. The tree house, and being with Mary Kay right now, and her thinking I was smart, and not even seeming to notice I was way shorter than her, and not dressed so good, either.

The stars above us made the universe look so immense. That's when I had the weird feeling. That good could come from bad, and that maybe I was being looked after by the same thing that put the stars in the sky, and that maybe everything was going to be okay.

It's the first time in my life I've ever felt that way. Like I didn't have to look after anything at all.

And all that was nothing compared to what happened later. Believe me, my uncle Ben and Miss Maple were about the furthest thing from my mind.

It was the first time Ben Anderson had had an evening to himself since Kyle had become a permanent part of his life. At first, watching his nephew go down the walk in front of the house and get into an upscale SUV, Ben felt heady with freedom.

He cocked his head and listened. No steady thump of the bass beat from down the hall.

"I could rent a movie, with bad language and violence," he said out loud, contemplating his options. "Man stuff." He beat his chest to get in the mood for man stuff, something he'd refrained from doing to avoid being scoffed at by his roomie.

Strangely, he discovered he could feel ridiculous all by himself. It was the influence of the annoying Miss Maple. Somehow, even though he was all alone, he could just picture her eyebrows shooting up at chest beating.

"I'll show her," he decided. "I'll call Samantha." But before he got to the phone he found his steps slowing at the thought of an evening with Samantha, pretty as she was. He'd given up on her even before Miss Maple, so imagine how dumb he'd find her now that he had someone to compare her to. Someone who could quote Aristotle, no less!

"Okay," he said. "Hillary, then." But Hillary hadn't had a moment of wonder for at least twenty-five years, and he didn't feel in the mood for worldliness or cynicism.

Pam had always been light-hearted, but he knew he'd find her giggling grating after the day Miss Maple had been hi-jacked by the compactor and he had heard her laughter. And seen her crinkle her nose.

"Okay," he said, annoyed with himself. "I'll call the guys."

But lately the guys were on a campaign to get him back in the game, as they called it, and the very thought of that made him feel more tired than a day of pouring concrete.

The truth was, once he stopped talking out loud, Ben

thought the house felt oddly empty without Kyle. Ben had become accustomed to the bass boom in the background, the squeak of the refrigerator door, the feeling of being responsible for something other than himself.

For a man who had never even succeeded at looking after a houseplant, the fact that he had taken to his guardian duties was a surprise.

Maybe he was maturing. Becoming a better man.

But then he thought of how he'd behaved this afternoon at Beth Maple's, and he didn't feel the least bit proud of himself.

"I think I will rent a movie," he said out loud, and reached for his jacket. At the movie store he picked up *Jackals of the Desert* a movie with a military theme, and a rating that would have never allowed him to watch it with Kyle, even though Kyle rolled his eyes at his uncle's adherence to the rating system.

But before he got to the cash register, he turned around and put the movie back on the shelf. There, under the bright lights of the video store, Ben faced the truth about himself.

He was trying to run away, fill space, so that he didn't have to look at an ugly fact about himself.

He'd hurt her. He'd hurt Miss Maple.

And he'd done it because telling her his sister was not going to make it, and feeling her hand rest, ever so slightly on his arm, had made him come face-to-face with a deeply uncomfortable feeling of sadness about his sister, and vulnerability toward Beth. He didn't want to face his feelings. He didn't actually even want to *have* feelings, messy, unwieldy things that they were.

So, not facing his feelings was nothing new, but hurting someone else?

Not okay.

Especially not okay because it was her.

By taking on the tree house project, Ben was trying to repair the damage that had been done to her, not cause more.

All she'd done was touch him when he'd told her Carly wasn't going to make it. But something in that touch had made him feel weak instead of strong. As if he could lay his head on her lap, and feel her fingers stroking his hair, and cry until there were no more tears.

No wonder he'd lashed out at her. *Cry?* Ben Anderson did not cry. Still, he could now see that it had been childish to try to get his power back at her expense.

"Man up," he'd said to Kyle when Kyle had been trying to shirk from the damage he had caused.

Now it was his turn.

He went out of the video store, and was nearly swamped by the smell of fresh pizza cooking. He hadn't eaten yet.

And that's how it was that he showed up on Beth Maple's doorstep a half an hour later with a Mama Marietta World-Famous Three-Topping Pizza and a six-pack of soda.

Beth opened the door, which gave him hope, because she'd peeked through the security hole and clearly seen it was him. But then she had folded her arms over her bosom like a grade-five teacher who intended not to be won over by the kid who had played hooky.

She was wearing a baggy white shirt and matching pants, that sagged in all the wrong places. Pajamas?

The outfit of a woman who did not get much company of the male variety by surprise.

And that gave him hope, too, though what he was hoping for he wasn't quite ready to think about.

So he thought about why he had come.

"Peace offering," he said, holding out the pizza box so she could see the name on it. Nobody in Cranberry Corners could resist a Mama's three-topping pizza. "And apology."

"Where's Kyle?" she said, peering into the darkness behind him.

"No Kyle tonight." And lest she think he was an irresponsible guardian, he said, "Kyle's at the planetarium, with Mary Kay somebody."

"Ah. I have to say I didn't see that one coming. Or this one."

She was speaking to him. After he'd been thoughtless and cruel and insinuated no one would break down a door to kiss her.

"Are you going to let me in?"

"I'm going to think about it."

"You know something, Miss Maple? There's such a thing as thinking too much."

"Probably not a problem in your world, Mr. Anderson."

"Not generally."

And then her lips twitched, but she still didn't open the door.

"Okay," he said, "I'm getting the fact that somehow you are finding me resistible, but Mama's pizza? Three-topping? Come on."

"What three toppings?" she said.

"Mushroom, pepperoni and the little spicy sausages."

He could see her weakening at the mention of the sausages. Which under different circumstances could be quite insulting to a man like him. She could keep the door shut to him, but not sausages?

"There have to be some rules in place," she said.

"There's such a thing as too many rules, too."

"There's the whole thing about dating family members of my students."

"This isn't a date!" he protested. "It's a pizza."

"Well, there is the complication of the kissing that you brought up earlier." She blushed when she said it.

"Okay," he grumbled. "I won't bring up kissing."

"You can't even think about it. Since we are unchaperoned this evening."

"Miss Maple, you cannot control what I am thinking about!" Especially now. Because she'd mentioned it, and his male mind had locked in on the delicate curve of that puffy bottom lip.

Suddenly this whole thing seemed like a really stupid idea. What had he come here for?

To make amends or to steal kisses? What did you do with a gal like Miss Maple once the pizza was gone? Play chess? Who on earth used the word *unchaperoned* if they were over the age of twenty-one?

"Look, I'll just leave the pizza. With an apology. I'm sorry if I hurt your feelings this afternoon. By insinuating a man wouldn't break down your door to kiss you. Because the right man probably would." He was making a mess of this somehow.

"You just said you weren't going to bring up kissing!" she said.

"But then you said I couldn't even think about it.

Which is ridiculous." What man wouldn't think about it in close proximity to those lips? "Miss Maple, there's an elephant in the middle of the room. We can't just pretend it's not there. Maybe we should just get it over with."

"What?" she squeaked. "Get *what* over with?"

He sighed. He couldn't believe he'd actually said that out loud. "Do you want to share the pizza with me or not? It's getting cold. I'm not asking you if you want to build a cabin in the wilderness with me and have my babies, for God's sake, just because I find your lips, um, provocative."

"I don't think it's wise for you to come in," she said.

"I agree, but let's live dangerously."

She contemplated that, as if inviting him in would rate as the most dangerous thing she had ever done.

He better remember that when he was looking sideways at her damn provocative lips. She didn't know the first thing about how to handle a man like him, despite her claim that her door had been knocked down for kisses before.

He actually wondered if he should do it. Just knock the door down and kiss her, so she could see it was not what she feared.

Except he had a feeling it might be more than he feared. If you kissed someone like her, you'd better not do it lightly, without thinking things all the way through to the end. That was the problem with him, and most men, no impulse control. Act now, pay later.

A little cabin in the woods filled with her and their babies didn't seem like such a terrible consequence.

The thought nearly sent him backward off her step, nearly sent him running for the truck.

Except, the door squeaked open.

"Behave," she told him in her sternest, grade-five-teacher voice.

"Yes, Miss Maple," he said meekly.

He reminded himself as he stepped over her threshold that he had come here to make things better, not worse.

Her inner sanctum was as he had known it would be, and it made him feel big and clumsy and menacingly masculine. There were ceramic vases on the floor, where they could easily be toppled by a wayward size-eleven foot. There was a huge clear-glass bowl with real flowers floating in it right on the coffee table in front of her television. One too-enthusiastic cheer for a touchdown and it would be goodbye flowers. And bowl. Probably coffee table, too, flimsy-looking thing on skinny, intricate legs.

Beth's was clearly a world for one: everything in its place, and everything tidy. Despite the fact the breakability factor made him somewhat nervous, there was nothing sterile or uptight about her home. Her space was warmed by tossed cushions and throw rugs, the walls were bright with beautifully framed artwork from her students.

She cast a look at her white slip-covered sofa, decided against it—whether because pizza and white didn't go together, or because it looked too small to hold two people who were going to behave themselves, he wasn't quite sure.

He did notice on the way through that this house was loved: hardwood reclaimed, moldings painted, windows shining. She led him through to the kitchen. It still smelled of the cookies she had baked that afternoon.

"What were you doing?" he asked, when she hurried over to the stove and shut off the burner.

"Making soup and doing a crossword puzzle. The soup couldn't compete with the pizza."

He stopped himself from asking how he compared to the crossword puzzle. It was still out, on a teeny kitchen table that could barely accommodate one, though there were two fragile chairs at it, with skinny, intricate legs that matched those on her coffee table. There were fresh flowers on that table, as well, and he was willing to bet she had bought them for herself.

The tinyness of the table, the crossword puzzle and the flowers were all stern reminders to him to behave.

She had a life she liked. She was the rarest of things. A person content with her own company and her own life.

"I'll help you with the puzzle," he decided, and took a careful seat. Did the chair groan under his weight?

He handed her the pizza since the table was not big enough to accommodate the box. He didn't miss the fact she raised an eyebrow at him, but took the pizza, and got them plates.

"Knife and fork?" she asked him.

"Get real." He squinted at the crossword puzzle. He should have known. It was one of the really hard ones, not like the sports one that came with the weekly TV guide in the local paper, which had supersimple clues like "Who is the most famous running back of all time?"

Out of the corner of his eye, he saw her setting a knife and fork on one of the plates.

"No utensils or I'll take my pizza and go home. Pizza is food you eat with your hands." *Loosen up*, he wanted to tell her. But then he wasn't so sure he wanted her to loosen up, especially when she complied with his instructions and brought over two plates, no utensils. She picked up her slice gingerly and took a tiny bite, then licked a wayward speck of sauce off her index finger.

He was not so sure he should have encouraged her. Watching Miss Maple eat pizza with her hands was a vaguely erotic experience, nearly as bad as watching her eat tiger ice cream.

He reminded himself they were unchaperoned. He was not even allowed to *think* anything that was vaguely erotic.

So, he concentrated on the crossword book. "A six-letter word for *dumb?*" he asked her, but spelled in his head *B-e-n*.

"Stupid?"

He scorned the pencil she handed him and picked up a pen off the table. "Nitwit."

"You can't fill it out in pen!" She didn't look too happy about him touching her book while he was eating, either.

"We're living dangerously," he reminded her. "I'll buy you a new book if I get pizza on it."

"I wasn't worried about my book!" she said huffily.

"Yes, you were. What's a seven-letter word for *hot spot?*"

"Volcano? I wasn't worried about the book."

"Yes you were. *Hell,*" he said, pleased.

"Hell does not have seven letters!"

"Hellish, then," he wrote it in, pressing hard on the pen so she wouldn't get any ideas about erasing it later. "Eight-letter word for *aggravation?*"

"Anderson?" she said sweetly.

How did she count letters so darn fast? "Perfect," he said approvingly, and wrote it in. "This is too easy for us. Next time the *New York Times.*"

Next time. Way to go, nitwit.

But somehow the evening did become easy. As they focused on the puzzle, she lost her shyness. She even was eating the pizza with relish. Her wall of reservation came down around her as she got into the spirit of wrecking the puzzle.

"Incognito," she crowed.

"It doesn't fit."

Impatiently she took the pen from him, scowled at the puzzle and then wrote, *"Inkono."*

"Miss Maple, you are getting the hang of this," he said with approval. "That makes *zuntkun* down."

"Zuntkun," she said happily, "a seven-letter word for an exotic horned animal in Africa if I'm not mistaken."

"Done," he declared, half an hour later looking down at the mess of scribbles and crossed-out words and wrong words with complete satisfaction. So was most of the pizza. So was his control.

This close to her, he could smell lavender and vanilla over the lingering scent of pizza. He liked the laughter in her eyes, and the crinkle on her nose. He decided to make both deepen. He ripped the puzzle out of the book.

"What are you doing?"

"It's a little something on you. From now on I have this to show your class how their teacher spells *incognito* in a pinch. If you make me happy, I'll never have to use it."

"How would I make you happy?" she asked warily.

"Use your imagination. Any woman who can spell *incognito* like that, and who can invent horned beasts in Africa, has to have a pretty good imagination."

"I have a better idea. Just give it back."

"I'm not one of your fifth-graders. I don't have to do

things just because you say so. You come get it," he teased, and at the look on her face he pushed back his chair.

She moved toward him. "Give it!"

"Don't make me run," he said. "You have highly breakable bric-a-brac."

She lunged at him. He turned and ran, holding the puzzle out in front of him. She chased him out of the kitchen and through the living room, around the coffee table and over the couch. The vases on the floor wobbled as he thundered by, but did not break.

She backed him into a corner up the hallway, by her open bedroom door. Decorated in many, many shades of virginal white. Unless he was going to mow her over, or move into her bedroom, which was out of the question, he was trapped. And delightfully so.

"Surrender," she demanded, holding out her hand.

"Surrender? As in nine-letter word for *give up?* Not in the marine vocabulary."

She made a snatch for it.

He held the puzzle over his head. "Come and get it," he said, and laughed when she leaped ineffectually at him.

Her face was glowing. She looked pretty and uninhibited and ferociously determined to have her own way. After several leaps, she tried to climb up him.

With her sock feet on top of his sock feet and her full length pressed against him, she tried to leverage herself for the climb up him. With one arm around his neck, and one toe on his knee, she reached for the paper, laughing breathlessly, her nose as crinkled as a bunny's.

She suddenly realized what she was doing. He wondered if it felt as good for her as it did for him. She went very still.

And then backed off from him so fast she nearly fell over. He resisted the impulse to steady her.

"Hmm," he said quietly. "That made me happy. Your puzzle is safe with me, for now. Unfortunately, I have to go." He looked at his watch. "Kyle will be home soon. I don't want him to come into an empty house. I think there's been a little too much of that in his life."

"You're a good man, Ben Anderson," she said.

He felt the mood changing, softening, moving back to where it had been this afternoon when she had laid her hand on his arm and he had felt oddly undone by it.

So he waggled the puzzle at her, eager to keep it light. Maybe even hoping to tempt her to try and climb up him one more time to retrieve it.

"I'm not really a good man," he said. "I have the puzzle, and I'm not afraid to use this. Don't forget."

"I'll see you to the door," she said, not lured in, and with ridiculous formality, given that she had just tried to climb him like a tree. She preceded him to it, held it open.

"Thank you for the pizza." Again the formal note was in her voice.

"You're welcome."

He stood there for a minute, looking at her. *Don't do it*, he told himself. She wasn't ready to have her world rattled. She wasn't ready for a man like him. There was no sense complicating things between them.

But, as it turned out, she made the choice, not him. Just as he turned to go out the door, he felt her hand, featherlight, on his shoulder. He turned back, and it was she who stood on her tiptoes and brushed her lips against his.

It was like tasting cool, clean water after years of

drinking water gone brackish. It was innocence, in a world of cynicism. It was beauty in a world that had been ugly. It was a glimpse of a place he had never been.

So the truth was not that she was not ready for a man like him. The truth was that he was not ready for a woman like her.

Who would require so much of him. Who would require him to learn his whole world all over again. Who would require him to be so much more than he had ever been before.

"Well," she said, stepping back from him, her eyes wide, as if she could not believe her own audacity, "I'm glad we addressed the elephant."

But he wasn't so sure. The elephant had been sleeping contentedly. Now that they had "addressed" it, they couldn't go back to where they had been before. Now that they had "addressed" it, it was going to be hungry.

Now that they'd addressed it, her lips were going to be more an issue for him, not less.

The elephant was now taking up the whole room instead of just a corner in the shadows, swaying sleepily on its feet, not being too obtrusive at all.

She leaned toward him again, and he held his breath. If she kissed him again, he was not going to be responsible for what happened next. Didn't she know the first thing about men?

But then she snatched the paper he'd forgotten all about from his hand, and laughed gleefully. Maybe she knew more about men than she had let on. She had certainly known how to collapse his defenses completely.

"Good night, Ben," she said sweetly.

And all the way home he brooded about whether she

had just kissed him to get her hands on that damned puzzle. He was still brooding about it when Kyle came through the front door.

He stopped brooding and stared at his nephew. Kyle was *shining*.

"Uncle Ben," Kyle said breathlessly. "What does it mean when a girl kisses you?" And then, without waiting for an answer, "I guess she likes you *a lot*, huh?"

Ben contemplated that for a minute, and then said, "I guess she does." *Either that or she wants something, like her puzzle back.*

CHAPTER SIX

SHE'D actually kissed Ben Anderson, Beth thought, as she put the leftover pizza in the fridge and the pizza box in the garbage.

Oh, no, not just kissed him, but *instigated* the kiss.

"What's that about?" she asked herself. Well, he'd encouraged her. "Live dangerously," he'd said.

Not wantonly, she chastised herself, *floozy*. And then she laughed at herself. Wantonly? Floozy? In this day and age a kiss like that wouldn't be considered wanton. It wouldn't make a woman a floozy.

She was twenty-five years old and she'd dared to brush lips with a man so attractive he made her heart stand still. She was glad she'd done it. She felt no regret at all. In fact, Beth Maple felt quite pleased with herself. There was something about being around him that made her want to be a different person.

Not reserved. Not shy. Not afraid. Not hiding from life.

She wanted to be a person who did the crossword all wrong and admitted it was so much more fun than doing it right. She uncrumpled her hard-won prize and looked at it, then moved into her kitchen and used a magnet to put it in a place of honor on her fridge.

The new Beth would break rules. The new Beth would not wait for a man to kiss her, but would kiss him if she felt like it.

She contemplated the experience of touching her lips to his and felt a quiver of pure pleasure. Imagine. She had almost gone through life without kissing a man like that! What a loss!

Ben Anderson had tasted even better than she could have hoped. It was as if the walls around her safe and structured little world had crumbled to dust when she had touched her lips to his.

Something was unleashed within her, and she wasn't putting it away. The old Beth would have worried about the awkwardness when she saw him again. But the new Beth couldn't wait.

She was *alive*. She had been sleeping, deliberately, ever since the fiasco with Ralph/Rock. She'd been wounded and had retreated to lick her wounds. She had convinced herself she was retreating for good.

And then, as if the universe had plans for her that she could not even fathom, along had come Kyle, and then his uncle, and then a tree house in her backyard, all the events of the past weeks beckoning to her, calling to her.

Live. She needed to live. Even if it was scary. She needed to embrace the wonderful, unpredictable adventure that was life. Not just live, she thought, but live by Ben's credo: *dangerously*.

Hilarious to have a turning point over a crossword puzzle, but Ben had shown her that. Have *fun*. Throw out the rules from time to time.

Now it was Sunday morning, and his truck pulled

up in front of her house, and he got out. Was his glance toward her window wary? As if he didn't know what to expect?

That was good, because she had a sneaking suspicion that in the past he was the one in control when it came to relationships. He was the one who decided what was happening and when.

Ben Anderson, she said to herself, *you have met your match*. And then she contemplated that with wicked delight.

A week ago she would not have considered herself any kind of match for Ben Anderson.

For a moment caution tried to rear its reasonable head. It tried to tell her there was a reason she had not considered herself any kind of a match for him. Because he was obviously way more experienced than her. She didn't really know him. They were polar opposites in every way.

But below the voice of reason, another voice sang. That it had seen how he was with his nephew, how calm and responsible and willing to sacrifice that he was. And it had seen his vision for her backyard taking shape, his plan, that whimsical tree house speaking to her heart and soul, as if he also saw the things about her that no one else did. Just as she had seen *him*, pure and unvarnished, when he talked about his sister.

And then, when she had kissed him last night she had tasted something on his lips.

Truth. His truth. Strength and loneliness. Playfulness and remoteness. Need and denial of need.

He had already strapped on his tool apron when she came out the door with hot coffee for him and a hot chocolate for Kyle. He took his coffee, said good morning, gruffly, as though they were strangers, but his eyes strayed to her lips before they skittered away.

"Guess what?" Kyle told her. "Mary Kay and I went to the planetarium last night."

"And how was that?" she asked.

"Awesome," he breathed.

She saw in him what she had always wanted for him, a capacity to know excitement, to feel joy, to be just an ordinary kid, a boy moving toward manhood, who could have a crush on a girl and still love tree houses at the very same time.

She glanced at Ben, and knew he saw it, too, and saw the incredible tenderness in his eyes as he looked at Kyle.

And she knew he could say whatever he wanted, but she would always know what was true about him.

"Could I bring her here and show her the tree house?" Kyle asked. "When we're done?"

"Of course," Beth said.

"It's not going to get done if we stand around here, drinking coffee," Ben said, and set his down deliberately. "Kyle, you can start hauling lumber from the truck for the platform. Stack it here."

Ben looked like he intended to ignore Beth, but she had a different idea altogether. She had found an old tool belt in the basement, and she strapped it on, too, picked up some boards and headed for the stairs.

"What are you doing?" he asked.

"I'm helping."

"You don't know anything about building a staircase," he said with a scowl.

"Well, you didn't know anything about crossword puzzles, either."

"We don't want *this* to end like *that*," he said. "Building things isn't like doing a crossword puzzle. There's a purpose to it."

"There's a purpose to crossword puzzles," she told him dangerously.

"Which is?" he said skeptically.

"They build brain power."

"But nobody gets hurt if they're done wrong. If we don't build this right, you could be up there in your hammock on a sunny summer day, sipping lemonade and reading romance novels, and the whole thing could fall down."

"Romance novels?" she sputtered. Had she left one out last night, or was she just that transparent?

"It's just an example."

He saw her as a person who had filled her life with crossword puzzles and fantasies! And annoyingly it wasn't that far off the mark!

But she was changing, but that made her wonder if it was true that nobody was going to get hurt from doing the crossword puzzle wrong. She was open in ways she never had been before, committed to living more dangerously. Rationally, that was a good way to get hurt.

She didn't feel rational. She felt as if she never cared to be rational again!

"Show me how to hammer the damn steps down, and how to do it so that I and my lemonade and my romance novel don't end up in a heap of lumber at the bottom of this tree," she told him.

"Ah, ah, Miss Maple. Grade-five teachers aren't allowed to say *damn*."

"You don't know the first thing about grade-five teachers," she told him.

His eyes went to her lips, and they both knew he might know one thing or two. He hesitated and then surrendered, even though it wasn't the marine way. "Okay, I'll put the stringers and then show you how to put the treads on."

In a very short while, she wondered how rational it had been to ask. Because they were working way too closely. His shoulder kept touching hers. He covered her hand with his own to show her how to grip the hammer. She was so incredibly *aware* of him, and of how sharing the same air with him seemed to heighten all her senses.

Alive. As intensely alive as she had ever been. Over something so simple as working outside, shoulder to shoulder with a man, drinking in his scent and his strength, soaking his presence through her skin as surely as the beautiful late-summer sunshine.

Before she knew it, they were at the top of the staircase.

"It's done," she said.

"Not really. At the moment, it's a staircase that leads to nowhere."

Trust a man to think that! It showed the difference between how men and women thought. He so pragmatic. She so dreamy. Amazing he had thought of the tree house in the first place!

Just to show him the staircase led to somewhere, she stepped carefully off the stair and onto a branch.

"Hey, be careful."

She ignored his warning, dropped down and shinnied out on the branch. From her own backyard was a view she had never seen before.

"I can see all of Cranberry Corners," she said. "This is amazing."

And that's what happened when you took a chance and lived on the edge. You saw things differently. Whole new worlds opened to you.

"You better come back here."

She ignored him, pulled herself to sitting, dangled her feet off the branch, looked out the veil of leaves to her brand-new view of the world and sighed with satisfaction.

"If you fall from there, you're going to be badly hurt," he warned.

She looked back at him. He looked very cross. Too bad.

"In between romance novels, I try and squeeze in a little reading that has purpose. Do you know Joan of Arc's motto?" she asked him.

"Oh, sure, I have Joan of Arc's motto taped to my bathroom mirror. What kind of question is that? Come down from there, Beth. Now is no time to be quoting Joan of Arc."

"'I am not afraid,'" she said, wagging her legs happily into thin air, "'I was born for this.'"

"Hey, in case you don't remember, Joan's story does not have a happily-ever-after ending."

"Like my normal reading?" she asked sweetly.

"It's not attractive to hold a grudge. I'm sorry I insinuated you might just read something relaxing and fun in between studying Aristotle. Get off that branch."

She glanced at him again. He did look sincerely worried. "You're the one who likes to live dangerously," she reminded him.

"Yeah. *Me*."

"You've encouraged me."

"To my eternal regret. Beth, if you don't come back here, I'm going to come get you. I mean it."

"I doubt if the branch is strong enough to hold us both."

"I doubt it, too."

It was a terrible character defect that she liked tormenting him so much. Terrible. It was terrible to enjoy how much he seemed to care about her. Though caring and feeling responsible for someone were two entirely different things.

"Is it lunchtime yet?" Kyle called up the tree. "Hey, that looks fun, Miss Maple. Can I come up?"

"No!" she and Ben called together, and she scrambled in off the branch before Kyle followed her daredevil example. Ben leaned out and put his hands around her waist as soon as she was in reach. He swung her off the branch and set her on the top stair. But his hands stayed around her waist as if he had no intention of letting her go to her own devices.

"I'm safe now," she told him.

But his hands did not move. They both knew that she was not safe and neither was he, and that what was building between them was as dangerous as an electrical storm and every bit as thrilling.

He let her go. "I'll take Kyle and grab a bite to eat."

She knew he was trying to get away from the intensity that was brewing between them.

"No need," she said easily. "There's lots of leftover pizza."

And so even though surrender was not the marine way, she found Ben Anderson in her kitchen for the second time in as many days. The problem with having him in her space was that it was never going to be completely her space again. There would be shadows of him in here long after he'd gone.

And men like that went, she reminded herself. They did not stay.

And right now it didn't seem to matter. At all. It was enough to be alive in this moment. Not to analyze what the future held. Not to live in the prison of the past. Just to enjoy this simple moment.

"Microwave or oven?" she asked of reheating the pizza.

They picked the oven, and while they waited she mixed up a pitcher of lemonade and asked Kyle about the program at the planetarium.

"Hey," she said, catching a movement out of the corner of her eye. "Hey, put that back!"

But Ben had his prize. He held up the puzzle that she had tacked on her fridge the night before.

"Ah," he said with deep satisfaction, and folded it carefully. He put it in his pocket.

"That belongs to me," she said sternly.

"That's a matter of opinion."

"It was on my fridge! It's out of my book."

"My. My. My. I thought by fifth grade you'd learned how to share."

And then she couldn't help it. She was laughing. And he was laughing.

Kyle, giving them a disgusted look, gobbled down the leftover pizza. "Is there any dessert?" he asked.

"Kyle!" Ben said.

But she was glad to see the boy eating with such healthy appetite. Since she didn't have dessert, she said, "Let's not go right back to work. Let's take the bicycles down to Friendly's and have an ice cream."

"How many bikes do you have?" Ben asked, looking adorably and transparently anxious to keep her away from that staircase to nowhere and her perch on the tree branch.

"About half a dozen. I pick up good bikes cheap at the police auctions. Then if there's a kid at school who needs a bike, there's one available."

"You really have made those kids, school, your whole life, haven't you?"

He said it softly. Not an indictment, but as if he saw her, too. "You have a big, big heart, Miss Maple."

And he said that as if a big heart scared him.

"Ice cream," she said, before he thought too hard about their differences.

Kyle made a funny sound in his throat. "I don't want ice cream," he said. "You guys go. Without me."

"Without you?"

They said it together and with such astonishment that some defensiveness that had come into Kyle's face evaporated.

"I don't know how to ride a bike," he said, and his voice was angry even while there was something in his face that was so fragile. "And you know what else? I don't know how to swim, either. Or skate.

"You know what I *do* know how to do? I know how to stick a whole loaf of bread underneath my jacket and walk out of the supermarket without paying for it. I know they put out the new stuff at the thrift store on Tuesday. I know how to get on the bus without the driver seeing you, and how to make the world's best hangover remedy."

Suddenly Kyle was crying. "I'm eleven years old and I don't know how to ride a bike."

He said a terrible swear word before *bike.*

Beth stared at him in shocked silence. And then her gaze went to Ben. He looked terrified by the tears, but he quickly masked his reaction.

"Big deal," Ben said, with the perfect touch of casualness. Somehow, he was beside his nephew, his strong arm around those thin shoulders. "Riding a bike is not rocket science. I bet I can teach you to ride a bike in ten minutes."

Beth knew if she lived to be 103, she would never forget this moment, Ben's strength and calm giving Kyle a chance to regain his composure.

Ben met her eyes over Kyle's head, and she realized the whole thing was tipping over for her. The look in his eyes: formidable strength mixed with incredible tenderness shook something in her to the very core.

It wasn't about living dangerously.

It was about falling in love. But wasn't that the most dangerous thing of all?

"Ten minutes?" Kyle croaked.

"Give or take," Ben said.

Of course he couldn't teach Kyle to ride a bike in ten minutes.

"Are you in?" Ben asked her.

It wasn't really about teaching Kyle to ride a bike. It was about so much more. Going deeper out into unknown waters. Going higher up the treacherous mountain.

It was about deciding if she was brave enough to weave her life through the threads of his.

What were her options? Her life before him seemed suddenly like a barren place, for all that she had convinced herself it was satisfying. It had been without that mysterious element that gave life *zing*.

"I'm in," she said. And she meant it. She was *in*. Totally surrendering. She'd never been a marine, anyway. It was perfectly honorable for her to give in to whatever surprises life had in store for her, to be totally open to what happened next.

It was like riding a bike. There was no doing it half-heartedly. You had to commit. And even if you ended up with some scrapes and bruises, wasn't it worth it? Wasn't riding a bike, full force, flat-out, as fast as you could go, like flying? But you couldn't get there without risk.

They selected a bike for Kyle from her garage and took it out on the pavement in front of the house. Soon they were racing along beside him, Ben on one side, she on the other, breathless, shouting instructions and encouragement. Just as in life, they had to let go for him to get it. Kyle wobbled. Kyle fell. Kyle flew. They were so engrossed in the wonder of what was unfolding that no one noticed when ten minutes became an hour.

"I think we're ready for the inaugural ride," Ben finally said. "Let's go to Friendly's for ice cream."

"Really?" Kyle breathed.

"Really?" she asked. Friendly's was too far for a novice rider. There would be traffic and hills. Try out those brand-new skills in the real world?

Maybe there was a parallel to how she felt about Ben. Try it out in the real world, away from the safety of her yard and her world? She remembered last time she'd been at Friendly's with Ben, too.

He'd gotten up abruptly and left her sitting there, by herself, with a half-eaten ice cream cone!

It reminded her he was complex. That embracing a new world involved a great deal of risk and many unknown factors.

But again she looked at her choices. Go back to what her life had been a few short weeks ago? Where reading an excellent essay full of potential and promise had been the thing that excited her? Or where finishing a really tough crossword had filled her with a sense of satisfaction? Or where building a papier-mâché tree for her classroom had felt like all the fulfillment she would ever need?

Her life was never going to be the same, no matter what she did.

So she might as well do it.

"Let's go," she said.

They rode their three bikes down to Friendly's Ice Cream. And then, after eating their ice cream cones, instead of riding back to her place, they took the bike trail along the river and watched Kyle's confidence grow. He was shooting out further and further ahead of them now, shouting with exuberance when they came to hills, racing up the other side, leaving them in his dust.

"You go ahead," Ben said to him. "You're wearing me out. Me and Miss Maple are going to do the old people thing and lie under this tree until you get back."

There were miles of bike trails here and they watched him go.

"Are you sure he's ready?" she asked, watching Kyle set off.

"Yup."

"How?"

"Look at him. Have you ever seen a kid more ready to fly?"

They sat there, under the tree, enjoying the sunshine and the silence, the lazy drift of the river. They talked of small things: the tree house, the wonder of Friendly's ice cream, bicycles and kids.

Beth was aware of a growing comfort between them. An ease as relaxed as the drift of the river. But just like the river, how smooth it *looked* was deceiving. A current, unseen but strong, was what kept the water moving.

And there was an unseen current between them, too. An awareness. She was *so* aware of the utter maleness of Ben Anderson. She had seen the way the women in the ice cream parlor looked at him, knew the body language of the women who jogged by on the bike path.

The old Beth would have been intimidated by that. The old Beth would have thought, *He's out of my league.* Or *What would a guy like this ever see in me*?

But the new Beth had *played* with him, had done crosswords and eaten pizza with her hands and held a hammer and defied him by sitting way out on the branch of a tree. She liked being with him, and she was pretty sure he liked being with her, too.

"Do you want to kiss me again?" she asked, thrilled at her boldness.

"Miss Maple, do you know what you're playing with?"

"Oh, I think I do, Mr. Anderson. Look at me. Have you ever seen a woman more ready to fly?"

He hesitated, momentarily caught, and then he leaned toward her, and she saw his nostrils flare as he caught the scent of her. His eyes closed, and he came closer.

"Beth," he said, and her name on his lips right before he kissed her sounded exactly as she had known it would, like a benediction.

His lips touched hers, as light as a dragonfly wing. And she touched his back, felt again that delicious sense of coming home, of knowing truth about someone that was so deep it could never be denied.

But then the lightness of the kiss intensified. He took her lips, and she felt his hunger and his urgency, the pure male desire of him.

It occurred to her maybe she didn't know what she was playing with, at all, but the thought was only fleeting, chased away by intensity of feeling such as she had never known.

This was not a picket fence kind of kiss.

It was the kiss of a warrior. The claim. It was fierce and it was demanding, and she knew another truth.

A man like this would take all a woman had to offer. She would have to be as deep and as intense, every bit as strong as he was. With a man like this there would be few quiet moments in the safety of the valleys.

He would take you to the peaks: emotional highs that were as exhilarating as they were terrifying and dangerous.

You would go higher than you had ever been before.

And you could fall further than you had ever fallen.

Unless you could fly. And hadn't she just asked that of him, if he had ever seen a woman more ready to fly?

Only, now that she was here, standing on the precipice of flight or falling, she was not sure she could fly at all.

Was she strong enough? Hadn't she broken a wing?

"Gross."

Ben pulled away from her as if he had been snapped back on a bungee cord. Neither of them had expected Kyle's solo flight be quite so brief.

But there he was, sitting on his bike, glaring at them, looking pale and accusing. Ben jumped up, reached back for her and pulled her to her feet, put her behind him as if he was protecting her from the look on his nephew's face.

"It wasn't gross," he said evenly, and something in the warrior cast of his face warned Kyle not to go further with his commentary, and Kyle didn't.

Still, Beth could clearly see that Ben either regretted the kiss or regretted getting caught, and it was probably some combination of the two. Clearly, unlike Kyle's bike ride, her flight was not going to be solo. And flying with someone who had doubts would be catastrophic. If the choice would be hers to make at all!

"There are some swans on the river down there," Kyle said, obviously sharing his uncle's eagerness to move away from that kiss. "I wanted you two to see them. They're too pretty to see by yourself."

And in that she heard wariness and longing, as if Kyle was showing them all how they felt about this relationship.

There were things too pretty about life to experience it all by yourself.

But trusting another person to share them with you was the scariest journey of all. Things could get *wrecked* by following a simple thing like a kiss to the mountaintop where it wanted to go.

It did feel like you could fly. But realistically, you could fall just as easily.

Kyle was only eleven and he already knew that.

Beth felt her first moment of fear since she had adopted the new her. Ben studiously ignored her as he got back on his bike and followed his nephew down the trail. She followed, even though part of her wanted to ride away from them, back home, to her nice safe place.

Funny it would be swans she thought, gazing at them moments later, the absolute beauty of jet black faces and gracefully curving white necks.

Funny they would be swans when she could feel herself beginning the transformation from ugly duckling. It was a transformation that was unsettling and uncertain.

And being unsettled and uncertain were the two things Beth Maple hated the most.

The Top-Secret Diary of Kyle O. Anderson

When I came down that bike path and saw my uncle and Miss Maple kissing, I felt sick to my stomach. I've seen my mom do this. Along comes the kissing part, and she's looking for a place to put me where no one will know I'm around.

So, I waited. I thought, my uncle will give me ten bucks and tell me to go get some more ice cream, but he didn't.

We went and looked at the swans and then we went back to Miss Maple's house and worked on the tree house some more. They didn't touch each other or kiss in front of me.

Miss Maple gave me the bike to take home, and my uncle and I went riding again after supper.

It's easy to ride a bike. I asked him if it was just as easy to swim and to learn to skate and he said a man could do anything he set his mind to.

As if he thinks of me as a man.

"Is there anything you're scared of?" I asked him.

And he didn't say anything for a long time. And then he said, "There's something everyone is scared of."

But he didn't tell me what it was, and you know

what? I didn't want to know, because I bet whatever he's scared of is really, really bad, worse than Genghis Khan being at the gate and telling you to surrender or else.

I wish my uncle Ben wasn't afraid of anything, because it's been really easy, working on Miss Maple's tree house, and eating pizza and ice cream, and going out with Mary Kay to the planetarium, to think maybe there is a place where I can feel safe and maybe I've found it.

Ha, ha. It's always when you think you have something that it gets taken away. Always.

CHAPTER SEVEN

BETH Maple had kissed him. Twice. Ben was trying as valiantly as he knew how to be the perfect gentleman, a role he was admittedly not practiced at. That's why he'd gone over there in the first place last night. To do the gentlemanly thing. To apologize.

But he had still planned to keep his distance, treat her like his nephew's teacher. Even doing the crossword had been about teaching her the innocent fun of not being so uptight. Break a few rules, for God's sake.

But the lines had an unpredictable way of blurring around her, and that was without her learning to be less uptight and break some rules. That was without watching her eat ice cream again, or race along a bike trail, shrieking with laughter.

Who would have guessed she would be the one instigating something more, confusing his already beleaguered male mind with kisses?

There was a chance her first kiss had been strictly a ploy to get the puzzle, and considering that would have made his world less complex, he had been strangely wounded by the thought. But kiss number two had erased any suspicion he had about ploys. She hadn't even tried to get the crossword that he had taken from her fridge out of his front pocket when she'd kissed him under the tree by the river.

Thank goodness for that, because things were complicated enough without her getting grabby *there*. Not that she was the type, but twenty-four hours ago he would have laid money she wasn't the instigating-kisses type, either.

This was the problem with kisses: in his experience kisses led to the *R* word, as in a Relationship. And in his experience that never went well for him. Women wanted most what he least wanted to give. Intimacy. Time. Commitment. A chunk of him.

He wanted a good time, a few laughs, nothing too demanding on his schedule, his psyche or his lifestyle. Which probably explained why a relationship for him, beginning to end, first kiss to glass smashing against the door as he said goodbye and made his final exit, was about one month. On a rare occasion, two.

He felt strangely reluctant to follow that pattern with Beth Maple. She'd only been in his life for a few weeks, but when he thought of going back to life without her, no tree house, no crossword puzzles, no bike rides by the river, he felt a strange feeling of emptiness.

"Look," he said, taking the bull by the horns after they had wheeled the bikes back into her garage. Kyle was out of earshot, loading up the tools in Ben's truck. They had made dismally little headway on the tree house today, which was part of why he had to take the bull by the horns. "We have to talk about this kissing thing."

"We do?" She had that mulish look on her face, the

same one she'd had as she was dangling her feet off a tree branch thirty feet in the air, the one that clearly said she wasn't having him call the shots for her.

"It's not that I don't like it," he said. He could feel his face getting hot. Hell. Was he blushing? No, too much sun and wind today.

"You don't?" she said sweetly, determined not to help him.

"I like it," he snapped, "but you should know I have a history with relationships that stinks. And that's how a relationship starts. With kissing."

"Thank you for the lecture, Mr. Anderson. Will there be a test?"

"I'm trying to reason with you!"

"You're trying to tell me you don't want to have a relationship with me."

"Only because it would end badly. Based on past history."

"Would you like to know what very important element was probably missing from your past relationships?"

Don't encourage her, he thought. It was obvious to him she was no kind of expert on relationships. Still, he'd come to respect her mind.

"What?" he asked.

"Friendship."

He stared at her. How could she know that? And yet if he reviewed all his many past experiences and failures, it was true.

He had never ever chosen a woman he could have been friends with.

And there was a reason for that.

He'd had his fill of hard times and heartaches. He'd

known more loss by the time he was twenty-one than most people would experience in a lifetime.

He'd become determined to have fun, and he'd become just as determined that the easiest way to stop having fun was to start caring about someone other than himself.

"We can be friends or we can be lovers," he said with far more firmness than he felt. "We can't be both."

He could tell by the shocked look on her face she hadn't even considered that's where kisses led.

"Wow," she said. "You know how to go from *A* to *Z* with no stopping in between."

Well put. "Exactly."

She looked at him for a long time. He had the feeling Beth Maple saw things about him that he didn't really want people to see.

She confirmed that by saying, "You know, Ben, you strike me as somebody who needs a friend more than a lover."

He wanted to tell her he had plenty of friends, but that wasn't exactly true. Not *girl* friends. He told himself he'd gotten the answer he wanted, the answer that kept everything nice and safe, especially his lips. He told himself this would be a good place to leave it. But naturally he wasn't smart enough to do that.

"And what do *you* need?" He was surprised that he asked, more surprised by how badly he wanted to hear her answer. What if she said, "I need to have a wild fling where I learn to let down my hair and live up to what my lips are telling you about me"?

He held his breath, but he got the stock Miss Maple answer.

"I need not to get involved with a family member of one of my students. On a lover level."

She blushed when she said it. What a relief. She couldn't even say *lover* let alone invite him to have a wild fling with her.

Her cheeks, staining the color of the beets his mother used to can, told him a truth about her. And about himself.

A man could never take her as a lover. She was the kind of woman who required way more than a recreational romp in the hay, whether she knew that about herself or not. She was the kind of woman who needed commitment. He'd known that from practically their first meeting when she had tossed that word around so lightly!

She was the kind of girl who would never be satisfied with the superficial, who would demand a man leave his self-centered ways behind him.

To be worthy of her. Which he was pretty darn sure he wasn't.

Thank God.

"Well, I'm glad we got that sorted out," he said doubtfully.

"Me, too," she said.

"It's not that I didn't like kissing you."

"I understand."

"So, you won't kiss me again?" What had his life become? He was begging a very pretty woman not to kiss him!

For her own good. Maybe he was becoming a better man, despite himself.

"I'll do my best," she said solemnly. And then, just when he thought she totally got what he was trying to tell her, she giggled, tried to hold it back and snorted in a most un-Miss Maple way.

He scowled at her.

"Rein myself in," she promised, and then snickered again. "Wanton floozy. I didn't mean to throw myself at you."

"Nobody says things like that," he said, irritated. "Wanton floozy."

She was laughing and snorting in an effort to restrain herself. "Oh, you know us readers of romance novels."

"You know, that's another annoying thing about you—" besides the fact that she looked absolutely glorious when she laughed, and her nose wrinkled like that "—you have this mind like a computer, and you store away every single thing a person ever says to you for later use. Against them."

She finally got the laughter under control, thankfully. Though now that he thought about it, he was not sure he liked that thoughtful, stripping way she was looking at him any better.

"You know what else was missing from your past relationships? Besides friendship?"

It was very obvious she planned to tell him, whether he wanted to hear it or not. Which he didn't. At least not very much. He glared at her, folded his arms over his chest.

"Brains," she said, softly. "No wonder you were bored."

"I never said I was bored!" But he realized he had been. Every single time, after the initial thrill, bored beyond belief.

"Well, based on what you said about your past history, *someone* was bored."

"Relationships can end for reasons other than that."

She wasn't insinuating the other person had been bored with *him*, was she?

"Yes, that's true. Maybe you're a bad lover."

He opened his mouth to protest, but caught the gleeful twinkle in her eye, and snapped it shut again before he gave her more cause to laugh.

He wasn't sure he even wanted to be friends with her after all, he thought, a trifle sullenly. She saw way too much. And said too much.

But what choice did he have? He had to finish building her tree house. And Kyle was going to be in her class for another nine months or so.

Excuses. Because it really did seem like his life the way it had been before she came along was not what he wanted anymore.

He'd been lonely. He knew that now.

She had been right. He needed a friend. He needed a friend just like her. As long as they didn't go and wreck it all by changing it to something else.

Feeling as if he had just navigated a minefield where he had managed, just barely, not to get himself blown to smithereens, he retreated to his truck and drove home. When they got in the house, Kyle announced he was going to do his homework.

Ben decided it would be counterproductive to remind Kyle he didn't do homework. Instead he contemplated that development, and allowed himself to feel a moment's satisfaction about how *his* plan was working the miracle that hers had not. But maybe it was bike riding that had worked the miracle, and that had been her idea. Turned into a project in cooperation. An outing with a family feeling to it.

Maybe that was at the heart of the miracle. That feeling of family. Ben's wisdom in saying nay to the kisses was confirmed, though there was a sharp and undeniable tingle of regret that went with it every time he thought about it. Or her lips.

He was still contemplating that when the phone rang. Miss Maple's personal number on his call display. He hadn't even been away from the many and varied temptations of her for an hour! Once upon a time, he remembered he had *hoped* she would call him. But that was before he'd known how capable she was of shaking up his world.

Still, it was not reluctance he felt when he answered the phone, much as he knew it *should* be.

"I can call you now that we're friends, right?" she asked. "It's not against your rules, like kissing?"

He hoped she wasn't going to mention kissing at every opportunity, because the whole idea was he didn't want to think about it.

"Of course you can phone me at anytime," he said foolishly. The pathetic truth was he couldn't think of anything he'd like more than talking to her. And the phone was so safe. He didn't even have to see her lips.

"You don't see my calling you as being too forward? Bordering on wanton?"

"No," he said sharply, trying to disguise how much he was liking this. "Are you amusing yourself at my expense?"

"Of course not. Actually, I called about Kyle, so this is definitely not wanton."

"Definitely," he agreed, disappointed that she had called about Kyle, even though he did appreciate her concern for his nephew's well-being. Besides, what could be better? That was a nice and safe topic.

"He told me he was going to do his homework," he whispered into the phone. It occurred to him there was no one else in the world who cared about that except her. It made him feel an unwanted nudge of tenderness for her. "Try not to make too big a fuss when he turns it in tomorrow."

"Don't worry, Ben, I'm not insulted that you think you have to tell me how to conduct myself in my classroom."

"Don't be so prickly." So much for tenderness. Which was good, tender thoughts probably would lead directly back to lip thoughts.

"Don't be so overbearing."

Boy, he was glad he had decided against complicating things!

"I'm not overbearing," he growled.

"Just far too used to calling the shots?"

"I run my own business!"

"You can't run your personal life like your business."

Had he actually been slightly happy to see her number on the call display? Why? She was bossy, opinionated *and* prickly. Who was she to tell him how to run his personal life? As far as he could tell, she didn't have one.

But if he said that, he was probably going to end up on her doorstep with pizza, apologizing again. And that led to lips, too. Instead he said, "Was there a reason you called?"

"I've been thinking about Kyle not knowing how to swim," she said, moving on quickly from the topic of his overbearingness, which he was glad about, even though he might have liked to talk about her prickliness a little more.

"It really bothers me," she said.

And just like that they were beyond the prickliness to that other side of her, so soft it beckoned like a big feather bed on a cold winter's night.

"Me, too," Ben agreed, and then found himself adding, "It's like he hasn't had a childhood."

"It's never too late."

"It isn't?" he said skeptically.

"My mom and dad have an indoor pool. It would be a nice private place to introduce him to the water and give him a few pointers on swimming. Don't you think a public pool might be too humiliating?"

But his mind was stuck on the "her mom and dad" part.

He did not like meeting his female companion's parents. Of course, he had just finished making it clear to her she was not going to be his female companion in the way he generally had female companions. So why not?

It wasn't until the next night, after school, at her parents' very upscale house in the hills, that he realized why not.

Beth met them outside in the curved driveway and led them around to a separate pool building behind the main house, glassed in and spectacular. He was relieved to note there were no parents in sight.

She pointed him and Kyle to a place to change, spa-like and luxurious, and moments later he was in the pool, testing the depth of the water for Kyle, who looked scrawny, goose-bumped and terrified of this new experience.

And then Beth emerged from her own change room. She shuffled up to the edge of the pool, drowning in a too-large pure-white thick terry cloth robe, and then, looking everywhere but at him, she took a deep breath and dropped the covering.

He really hadn't needed to see a woman he had sworn off kissing in a bathing suit. He really hadn't needed to see that at all. Because Beth Maple, out of her school-marm duds was unbelievable. Oh, he'd seen hints of this in the way she dressed at home, casually, but nothing could have prepared him for Beth Maple in the flesh.

Literally.

He wouldn't have ever thought she was a bikini kind of gal. In fact, for the school outing he had guessed she would wear a one-piece *with* matching shorts, not removed. Wrong. Though, he had just enough wits about him to see that the shimmery copper-colored hanky she was wearing looked brand-new. It had never been at a school outing! Was she tormenting him, deliberately, with his choice to just be friends?

Surely not! There was nothing conniving about Miss Maple, was there?

Ha. She knew exactly the effect all those scantily covered curves would have on his resolve. Nobody was that innocent!

Proving her own boldness was making her at least as uncomfortable as it was him and that she had no experience with the fact that the kind of swimwear she was wearing was not actually designed for swimming, Beth dove headlong into the water. And came up with one arm crossed firmly across her chest, and the other tugging away at something he couldn't see—but could clearly imagine—below the water.

"Problems?" he purred.

Nope, those little scraps of fabric were definitely not attire designed to get wet. At least her hair made her look like a drowned rat instead of a femme fatale making a play for his soul.

"No," she snapped, but made some tightening adjustments to the little threads holding everything together.

Now satisfied everything was going to stay on, she soon forgot to be self-conscious about her attire. After a few minutes of waiting, hopefully, for things to fall apart, he began to realize the bathing suit proved to be not nearly as revealing as her absolute joy and freedom in the water.

Her enthusiasm was contagious, and soon she had Kyle in the water and doing what she called a "motorboat," blowing bubbles with his mouth to get him over his fear of getting his face wet.

Never once did she make it seem like a swim lesson. Kyle's first time in the pool was all about fun. She never asked him to get out of the three foot end of the pool.

The three of them splashed and played tag. She got out a volleyball for them to throw around. An hour passed in the blink of an eye.

The whole experience made Ben want to get her alone, to swim with her in the Pacific on one of those nights when the sky and the water became one. Was that something someone wanted to do with their friend?

They had no sooner gotten out of the pool than the moment Ben dreaded, meeting her parents, arrived. Her mom provided them all with thick white robes that matched the one Beth had come out on the pool deck in. She got sodas out of the fridge as they all plopped down on the comfy furniture in the poolside lounging area.

Ben didn't miss the way Beth's mother's eyes popped at her daughter's bathing suit before Beth managed to get herself covered up.

So, Miss Maple did have a conniving side! He'd bet his business that her bathing suit was brand-new and carefully chosen to fluster. Though at the moment, trying to tug an uncooperative robe over her wet skin, Ben was pleased to see she seemed to be the flustered one.

After a few minutes her father joined them.

Ben was good at meeting people, and because of his line of work he was not intimidated by wealthy people. Despite his reluctance to meet parents, he realized he didn't have to act like a high school kid picking up his prom date, because he and Beth were not dating.

Her parents were easy people to be with, but Ben became aware he had avoided this kind of gathering since the death of his parents. Mr. And Mrs. Maple were obviously devoted to their youngest child and each other. It soon became evident that family was everything to them, their lives were centered on their children and their grandchildren. It was the main reason they had a pool.

Family.

That thing he had turned his back on so long ago, because it filled him with such an intense sense of yearning for what he could never have back.

But with this family he let himself relax into it, found himself looking at Beth's silver-haired, slender, elegant mother, Rene, thinking, *Beth will look like this one day.* And he hoped she would have the same light in her eyes—the rich contentment of a woman well loved.

But his relaxation faded a bit when he realized he would probably never see her silver-haired. And a bit more when he thought Beth would probably also want this someday. Oh, not necessarily the pool, but what it represented. Family closeness, family gatherings, family having fun together.

Beth's dad, Franklin, thankfully, did not do the interrogation thing. Instead he shared his own memories of his military life, without probing Ben's.

A man used to grandchildren, he included Kyle with ease in the conversation, drawing him out of himself.

"It's good to know how to swim," he told Kyle when Kyle confessed he was just learning. "You never know when you're going to fall out of the fishing boat."

"I've never been fishing," Kyle said.

"Never fishing? That won't do, will it? I'm taking my grandson with me next weekend. He's about your age. Why don't you come?"

"Can I, Uncle Ben?"

Ben looked away from the hope shining in his eyes, tried to control the feeling that came with Beth's world opening up to include them.

Hope. She was steadily hammering a crack into the hard exterior of his cynicism, his protective shell. But she was drawing Kyle into her world, too. Was he going to be hurt in the long run?

Still, he could not say no to the light shining in Kyle's eyes.

Ben had meant for the no-kissing rule to put distance between him and Beth, to erect a much-needed barrier between them, to put ice on that heated flicker of physical attraction they both felt.

Instead, as a week turned into two, he could see it was having the exact opposite effect.

Here was the thing about the no-kissing rule. It gave him room to *know* her. He was falling more for her, not less. He had not been aware how immersion in the throes of passion could actually thwart the process of two people getting to know each other. What he had always foolishly called intimacy was anything but. Physical intimacy, too soon, was actually a barrier to the kind of emotional and spiritual intimacy he was experiencing on a daily basis.

He could talk to her in a way he had never talked to anyone. Not about the weather or football stats or the best pizza, but about things that mattered. Education, politics, local issues. He moved beyond the superficial with her and found their conversations a deeply satisfying place to be. She didn't always agree with him— well, hardly ever, actually—but he loved sparring with her, matching wits, debating. It felt as if she kicked his brain up into a different gear.

After a while, he noticed that in any particular moment he could read how she felt about the day or life or him in the set of her shoulders and the light in her eyes.

Ignoring the signs that something was happening to him, he got in deeper and deeper as his life seemed to revolve more and more around her. He always seemed to be at her place, working on the tree house or riding bikes after school. Twice a week they went to her parents' to use the pool. Kyle went fishing with her dad and made a new friend in her nephew, Peter.

Even his sister noticed that something was going on in the lives of her brother and her son. On one of their regular visits, her eyes followed Kyle as he went to the hospital cafeteria to get her a soda.

"He seems so happy," she said.

It was probably awful to think it, but his sister was a nicer person since being hospitalized. But without access to drugs and alcohol, she seemed to be becoming a better person every day.

But as her spirit became better, her physical body weakened.

"Who is Miss Maple?" she asked him, turning her attention back to Ben suddenly.

"His teacher."

"No, Ben, who is she to you?"

"Just a friend," he said, defensively.

Something old and knowing and wise was in his younger sister's face.

"I'd like to meet her."

As if their lives weren't tangled enough without Beth meeting his dying sister.

Ben was astonished how strongly he didn't want Beth to meet his sister.

Because he knew as easily as he now read Beth, she also read him with a kind of uncanny accuracy. Beth would know the truth. When it came to Carly, his heart was breaking.

And Beth might try to fix it, knowing Beth.

And the truth was he was not sure he wanted her to. Because a heart shattered beyond repair might be his last remaining defense.

Who is she to you?

It had all been well and good to spend more and more time with her, to pretend that not kissing her meant it wasn't going anywhere that he needed to worry about.

But his sister's question bothered him deeply. Because his heart answered instantly, even though his head refused to give it words.

Who is she to you? Everything.

But there was a problem with making one person everything, with investing too much in them. He left the hospital feeling as if he'd snapped awake after allowing himself to be lulled into a dream. He felt grim and determined. Even the friendship thing wasn't working.

They were going too deep. He was caring too much.

It was time to pull it all back, to gather his badly compromised defenses, to make decisions, rather than just floating along in the flow.

He knew what he had to do. Take back his life. Stop with all the distractions. No more swimming. Or bike riding. In fact, he would finish the tree house.

A nice way to end it. Give her that final gift and bid her adieu.

Though nothing ever quite went as he planned it with her. The kissing thing being a case in point.

Not everybody would have been as flattered as Beth Maple by a handsome man absolutely resolved not to kiss her. But the situation she was in was different than a man telling a woman he just wanted to be friends because he just wanted to be friends!

With that amazing gift of women's intuition, Beth knew Ben didn't want to kiss her because he had felt her sway over him. What had frightened him had empowered her. Imagine a guy like that being so terrified of a girl like her! It was probably very wicked to find his discomfort as entertaining as she did.

But as the last days of summer shortened into fall,

she could see the heady truth every day, deepening around them. Ben Anderson was afraid of how he felt. He was manly enough to be terrified of all his feelings, as if somehow liking a person and coveting their lips gave them the power and made him powerless.

So, she would respect his wishes, but it was only human to torment him, wasn't it? To make him want to kiss her so badly that he would throw his self-control to the wind.

Not that it had happened so far, but she was absolutely confident it was only a matter of time until Ben surrendered to what was sizzling in the air around them.

My goodness, Beth said to herself, astounded at her confidence, *You are a prim little schoolteacher. What makes you think you can bring a man like that to his knees?*

More important, what are you going to do with him once you have him there?

She continued to tangle their lives together as if the only consequences would be good ones.

Her parents adored him and Kyle. Kyle was becoming like a member of her large and loving extended family. If some professional line had been blurred there, it was worth it to see Kyle becoming so sure of himself, flourishing under the attention and care of her family.

This weekend, she thought, watching Ben's truck pull up in front of her yard, will be a turning point. Kyle was gone to spend the weekend at her nephew's house. She and Ben were going to be alone.

She went out to greet him, but faltered when the welcoming grin that she had become so accustomed to was absent. He barely looked at her as he grabbed his tool belt from the back of his truck, strapped it around his waist.

"I'm finishing the tree house tonight."

She froze in her tracks, hearing exactly what he was not saying. It was the thing that linked them together, the tree house was their history.

Some couples had a favorite song.

They had the tree house.

Of course most couples kissed. Of course he was as eager not to be a couple as she was to be one.

That's what finishing the tree house was about, she realized.

Not kissing had not worked. It had not put the distance between them that he had hoped.

He was going to start cutting the ties one by one. She had been confident in her ability to hold him, but now she could see his desire not to be held was fiercely strong. He feared what she longed for.

And she felt devastated by his fear.

But she reminded herself, fiercely, that she had more power than he wanted her to have. The woman she had been a month ago would have accepted the look on his face, the formidable set of his shoulders, resigned herself to the decision he was making.

But that was not the woman she was today. She was not letting him go, not without a fight.

Too soon, with the last of the daylight leeching from the air, Ben drove home the last nail. The tree house was done.

They stood side by side at the sturdy handrail, close, but not touching. She felt loss rather than accomplishment, and she was almost certain he did, too.

"It's too late to put in the plants that attract butterflies," he said. "I'll get you a list, so you can do it next spring. There's no sense hanging the hammock, either, you'll find it too cold to use it this year."

You. Not *we*. The distinction was not lost on her.

It was true September had somehow drifted into October. There was a chill in the air.

And in his eyes.

"Wait here," she said. "I have something." She went into the house and found a bottle of champagne she had purchased a long time ago, for the weekend that Rock had been supposed to come. The first of many where he had been supposed to come and then never showed up. Why had she saved it? So that she could look at it and pity herself more?

She climbed back up the stairs with the bottle and two fluted glasses and a determination to enjoy every sip. It could be symbolic of letting go of the past. Looking at him, though, she realized she had already let go of the past.

That was one of the gifts Ben had given her, and even if he went now, he could not take away the woman she had become because of him.

"Are you going to break that over the bow?" he said, but there was no twinkle in his eye the way there usually was when he teased her.

"No, I'm going to get drunk and fall off the platform."

The twinkle flashed through the deep green of his eyes, but it was reluctant. He did not want to get drawn into her world. Normally he would have had some comment, some comeback, but now he remained silent.

She uncorked the champagne with a dramatic pop, but was so aware the atmosphere was not celebratory.

It felt like an ending. The end of the season. The end of something that had been growing between them.

She filled the wineglasses, passed him one. He lifted his, held it up to her, his eyes met hers.

"To all your dreams coming true, Beth."

Not *ours*. *Yours*. He was definitely getting ready to say goodbye.

"What do you know of my dreams?" she asked him quietly, taking a sip of her champagne and looking out over her yard and her house, once the only dreams that she had dared to harbor.

He actually laughed, but it had a faintly harsh sound to it, bitter.

"Do you think I could spend this much time with you and not know about your dreams? You dream of having a feeling like your mom and dad have for each other, and a life like the one they have. You dream of a family and swings in the backyard."

"I don't!" she said stunned.

"Yes, you do," he said quietly.

"Maybe I did once," she tilted her chin up proudly. "But I gave it up."

"You thought you did. The lowlife only hurt you temporarily, which is a good thing to remember."

"What do you know about Rock?" she whispered. Had somebody told him? One of her family members? Good grief.

"Rock," he snorted. "The name alone should have sent you running for cover."

"Did somebody tell you?" she demanded.

"Oh, Beth, this told me." He swept the view of her yard, wineglass in hand. "The little house for one, a car babied more than a, well, baby. You told me all about your heartbreak just by being a buttoned-up teacher devoting her life to her students."

"How dare you make me sound pathetic!"

"I don't find you pathetic," he said, quietly and firmly. "Not at all. You just want things, Beth. It's not wrong to want them. But there's no point hanging out with a guy who can't give them to you."

She was stunned by what he was seeing, because she thought that was precisely what she had given up after Rock/Ralph. But now she saw that Ben had clearly seen her truth, maybe before she had completely seen it herself.

She had convinced herself she was just playing a game with Ben, seeing if she could overcome his aversion to caring for another. She had talked herself into thinking it was all about her reclaiming her power in the face of having lost it.

But underneath all those things she had been telling herself, the dream of love had been creeping back into her life, fueled by his laughter and the green of his eyes and his fun-loving spirit and his ability to suddenly go deep in unexpected and delightful ways.

He had seen her more clearly than she saw herself. And her secret motivations were what was driving him away, what had brought that look into his eyes, why suddenly he had felt an urgent need to *finish*.

"Well. Whether you think I'm pathetic or not I am. You know what I did? I fell in love over the Internet. Conservative, cautious me, taken for a ride. How's that for pathetic?" She could not believe she was crying, but she was and she couldn't stop talking, either, despite the fact her confessions were making her miserable.

Why was she telling him this now, when he had leaving written all over him? She hadn't become one of those women who would take pity if they couldn't have love, had she?

"It ended up he wasn't even a real person. He had stolen pictures from a Web site of a male model. This fraud was having relationships with dozens of women. I was contacted by an investigator in his state. Asking if I'd ever sent him money."

"Had you?" It was a deep growl of ferocious anger.

"I said I hadn't, because I felt so foolish for believing his stories. An inheritance tangled up in court. His pay cheque stalled by the bureaucracy in Abu Dhabi. He was always so sincerely embarrassed. But everyone had tried to tell me. My family. My friends. I wanted so desperately for what I was feeling to be true that I wouldn't listen.

"I told the investigators I hadn't given him money because I just wanted it over. I didn't want revenge, I didn't want my name to appear in lists of women who had been victimized by him."

"You know I'm going to kill him if I ever see him, right?" Somehow his arm was around her shoulder, and she was pulled in hard against the pure strength of him. It seemed like such a safe place. She kept talking, the flood gates refusing to be closed now that everything was gushing out of them.

"The strange thing is for the longest time after, it still felt as if he'd been real. I mourned Rock as though a real person had died."

"And now?"

Now I know real. I have you to thank for that. But

out loud she just said, "I can't believe I've wasted one more tear on him."

She found her face cupped in his hand. He dragged the tear away from her cheek with the rough edge of his thumb. Somehow his thumb ended up on her lip, and he was looking deep into her eyes, and she could see his resolve to be on his way melting.

"Come here," he said with a sigh, and he sat down on the planking of the deck and pulled her into him and held her between the vee of his legs. Home.

Wasn't that really what she'd longed for? What she had hoped to find when she had bought that tiny, run-down house?

But the house, in the end, was just sticks and stones. His arms around her felt like a shelter from the hurts of the world. She peeked up at his face. This is what she wanted to come home to.

A real man. Like him.

"I wish I could tell you life won't hurt you anymore," he said finally, quietly. "But I can't. It will. Life stinks sometimes."

"That's why you have to have places like this tree house," she said dreamily. *Places like his arms. Home*.

He said nothing.

"Ben?"

"Uh-huh?"

"Will you tell me? About that hurt inside of you?"

"Trading war stories?" he said. "No, I don't think so."

"Trading trust," she suggested. "Laying down the burden."

"Beth, I don't want to lay my burdens on you."

"You've carried them long enough."

"Beth," he said softly, "why is it you are determined to make me weak? When I am just as determined to be strong?"

"I guess I don't see a man speaking of the forces that shaped him as a weakness. A true form of courage. The ability to be vulnerable. To not be lonely anymore. Tell me."

He was silent; she held her breath. And then he spoke. A surrender.

"My parents were killed in a car accident when I was seventeen. We had a family like your family, only without the financial security. I mean, I didn't know that growing up. We always had everything. Good home, nice clothes, plenty to eat, money to play sports.

"But when my mom and dad died, I found very quickly that there was nothing. A big mortgage on the house, no insurance, no savings."

"Ben, what a terrible burden to add to the grief you must have been feeling."

"Sometimes I think that time was so desperate I postponed grief. I had to figure out quickly how to look after things. There was no question of being able to look after my sister, too.

"The marines took me. A good family for a guy who has just lost everything. Feelings are scorned in the rough camaraderie of men. I was given a new purpose and a new family, and I wasn't allowed to indulge my desire to immerse myself in misery.

"But Carly. Oh, Carly. She was so much younger than me. Fourteen is a hard age without adding the complication of a life unfairly interrupted by tragedy. My parents were gone, and I was going.

"Sometimes I can still hear her howling like a wounded animal when I told her I had to go to the marines. She was a dreamer. Somehow she thought we were going to make it together. She was going to quit school and get a job in a fast-food place, she thought I could get a job, too. Two underage kids on minimum wage, no health care, no safety net. I knew it wasn't going to work, but she hated me for knowing." He shook his head, remembering.

"She went from one foster home to the next, becoming more bitter and more hard and more incensed at the unfairness of her life by the day. She went wild, got pregnant. I don't know if she ever told the father, or if she told him and he just didn't care.

"I'm the last person she ever would confide in. She never ever forgave me for leaving her.

"The truth is I've never really forgiven myself. I look at her and think, Couldn't I have done something? Couldn't I?"

Beth felt the helpless heave of his shoulders.

"Aren't you doing something now?" she asked softly.

"It's too late. I can't save my sister."

"But you're saving Kyle."

"Beth," he said, and there was something tortured in his voice, "don't make me into a man I'm not."

"I think you're the one who wants to make yourself into a man that you're not. I see who you really are, Ben Anderson."

"You do, huh?" And there was that teasing note in his voice again, as if he had decided to stay, after all.

And something in her decided to risk it all.

She spoke the truth that she had just admitted to herself, "And I'm falling in love with who you really are."

She kissed him then, up there in the tree house, with the leaves looking so magnificent in their dying throes.

"That's what I was afraid of," he said against her lips.

"You don't have to be afraid anymore, Ben."

And she felt him surrender to her as he retook her lips with his own.

CHAPTER EIGHT

BEN Anderson had gone to Beth's house planning to *finish*. Everything. It disturbed him that even setting his formidable will to that plan, things had gone seriously awry.

Seriously.

The thing about Beth was that she had seen that he was flawed. She had seen right through his warrior bravado to the fear underneath it.

The fear of loss. He had a terror about caring for people. But Beth clearly saw the cause: the fear of loss.

The thing about Beth was that she saw all that he was, good and bad, strong and weak, and loved him anyway. He saw it in her eyes. That she knew completely who he was, and even knowing that, she was willing to take a risk on him.

The thing about Beth was she took a man worn right out on his own cynicism, a man who had been through the wars, on every level, and made him want to hope again for a better world and a better life, a life with soft places to fall.

Somehow, even though he had gone to her house with every intention of saying farewell to her and to the part of him that *hoped*, he had been unable to leave her. He'd been unable to walk away from that feeling of being connected. He had been seduced by the magic of that place among the leaves, by the look in her eyes, by the way it felt to have her leaning her back against his chest, as if she belonged there, and to him.

She had been right, as she so often was—one of her most annoying qualities. And endearing.

He had felt better after he had spoken of his history. Trusted her with it. He had felt not so alone in the world. Lighter.

Ben had felt connected to another human being in a way that he had lost faith that it was possible to be connected. Destiny had laughed at his resolve to leave her, to finish it. Instead, they had stayed in that tree house all night. Watching the sky turn that purple blue before blackness, watching the stars wink on above them through the filter of leaves that were turning orange and fire red, a reminder that seasons ended.

They had finished the wine, but instead of ending it there, he had acquiesced when she had gone and got blankets and coffee. And then more coffee, and somehow pink had been painting dawn colors in the sky, and they'd both been wrapped in the same blanket, her breath feeling like his breath, her heart beating at one with his heart.

Finally, when he had pulled himself away, it had not been with a feeling of things ending, but of a brand-new day dawning in every possible way.

He'd driven home, the effects of the wine long since worn off, but drunk nonetheless. On exhaustion. And the look in her eyes.

Drunk on the possibility that he loved her, and that maybe he was strong enough and brave enough to say yes to a beginning instead of an end.

But he of all men should have known. What had he said to her? Not very poetic, just truth, unvarnished.

Life stinks.

And wasn't it always when a man forgot that, that life was more than willing to remind him?

He had barely stripped off his clothes and climbed into bed when his phone rang. Who else would call at such a ridiculous hour of the morning? Who else would know he was not asleep? He reached for it eagerly, thinking, *It is her.* Thinking she had thought of one last thing to say to him before she, too, slept.

In that moment before he picked up the phone he had an illuminating vision of what his life could be. He could fall asleep with his nose buried in the perfume of her hair, with her sweet curves pressed into his. His last words at night could be to her, and his first ones in the morning.

She had said she was falling in love with him.

He was falling in love with her. There it was. The admission. And for the first time in a very long time he could see something different for himself.

Not a desire to run. But a desire to have a place to lay his head. A place to put down his armor. A place where he loved and was cherished in return.

"Hello." Everything in his voice greeted her, ready to tell her, ready to see where it all went.

Only, it wasn't her.

"Mr. Anderson?"

His heart plummeted. Something about the official sound of the voice, the sympathy underlying told him before he heard a single word. That he had hoped too hard for a happy ending.

Carly.

"You'd better come," the nurse told him gently. "It's a matter of hours."

Somehow, in a nightmare of slow motion, he managed to pull on his clothes. He ignored the impulse to call Beth, and instead phoned Peter's house to tell them he was coming for Kyle. His early-morning phone call there had woken the whole family, and when he arrived everybody had that pinched look of distress about them.

Kyle's shoulders were hunched, and he looked bewildered as he followed Ben out to the truck and got in beside him.

Ben wished he had called Beth. She would know what to do. She would, he reminded himself, also trust that he knew what to do.

"Are you okay?" he asked Kyle.

"No."

"Me, neither."

"I'm so scared," Kyle said.

"Me, too."

"Is this what you're scared of?" Kyle asked him, his voice a croak of fear and misery. "You told me once everybody was scared of something. Is this what you're scared of, Uncle Ben?"

Ben could barely speak over the lump in his throat. "Yeah," he finally said, "this is it." He knew his nephew thought he meant death, but he had dealt with more death than most people, and it was not that that scared him.

Love. It was love that scared him the most. Because

love always seemed to, in the end, cut a man off at his knees, prove to him how puny his will was against the way of the world.

And he had almost given himself over to the cruel vulnerability of loving again. Almost. Not quite.

Had it been Beth's voice on the phone this morning, his whole life could have been unfolding differently. But he quashed the yearning and vowed not to go there anymore.

Ben and Kyle made their way through the too-bright lights of the hospital hallways to Carly's room.

It was darkened after the hall, and Ben hesitated in the doorway, one hand on Kyle's shoulder as he let his eyes adjust to the light.

Had it been the right thing to bring his nephew here? He wished he had asked Beth. But the privilege of sharing her wisdom, of walking through life sharing his burdens meant he had to make a decision. He had made one in the dawn hours, with her warm in his arms, but with the ringing of the phone this morning he was reneging on it.

Was it right for him to have brought Kyle? He felt the loneliness of having to make these huge decisions alone, but he squared his shoulders, resolved. Ben had seen people die and it was a hard thing to see. But wouldn't it have been harder for his nephew not to have had this opportunity to say goodbye?

In the room his sister was the slightest little bump under a blanket, as if she had begun disappearing long ago. She turned her head to them, and in her face Ben saw no fear and no anguish.

Absolute serenity.

"Kyle," she whispered, "come here."

Kyle went to her, and despite her frailty he climbed on the bed and into her arms. She rocked him and kissed the top of his head. She told him over and over she loved him. She told him she wasn't the mother he deserved. She told him he was a good kid. She told him she was proud of him.

The tears slithering down Kyle's face puddled on her nightgown, soaked it. Ben tiptoed out of the room. This was the moment they needed, the moment Kyle had waited all his life for.

After a long time Kyle came out into the hallway, wiping his face on his sleeve.

"She wants to see you, by yourself."

"Are you okay?"

His nephew gave him a look.

"Sorry, dumb question." He chucked him on the shoulder, changed his mind and pulled him hard into his chest and then released him reluctantly and went into the room.

"You'll look after him, won't you, Ben?" Something so desperate in that, pleading.

"I promise."

She studied his face, seemed satisfied. "Don't tell him I said this, but I'm glad. I'm glad it's over. I missed them so much, Ben."

"I know."

"Could you hold me?" she whispered.

He slid onto her bed, and scooped her up in his arms. It was like holding a baby bird.

"You know what I missed the most? This. Cuddling with Mom or Dad. Hearing the words *I love you*. You never said them, you know? You'd bring food or toys for Kyle and me, but you never said that."

"I'm sorry."

"Me, too, Ben. So much regret. I've put everyone I ever cared about through hell. Don't let me go," she said, and her hand curled into his shirt, holding him tight to her. Slowly her grip on him relaxed.

Her eyes closed and her breathing rattled laboriously.

He knew what he was hearing. He knew she would not wake up again. At some point Kyle came back into the room, squeezed into the bed with them, laid his head on his mother's breast, allowed his uncle to curl his hand around his shoulder, holding them both.

At six o'clock that night, as normal families sat down to eat their supper and talk about who was driving the kids to Little League, his little sister, as frail as a tiny bird that had fallen from the nest, found peace at last.

But there was no peace for Ben. He realized, even in the end, he had not been able to give her what she needed the most. Shocked, he realized he had let his chance to say the words *I love you* slip away from him.

Now he knew why he had gone to Beth's house to finish it. Not to save himself. But to do the most loving thing of all: to save her from a man who had never been able to give anyone what they needed or wanted.

Three simple words.

I love you. A gift his sister had waited and waited for. And he had never given it. Not even as his chances ran out.

Beth deserved a man who was better than that. So much better.

CHAPTER NINE

BETH tried not to let her shock show when she saw Ben.
It was the first time she had seen him since his sister's
funeral, which had been over a month ago. She had
spoken to him on the phone several times, but there was
no mistaking the chill in his voice. She had failed to
tempt him back into her world. She could feel the formidable force of his will set against her.

Not her, personally, she reminded herself. His will
had become a defense against all the things that had
ever hurt him.

She had gotten him here to the school on the pretext
of a parent-teacher night, and she knew she had chosen
her own outfit—elegant silk blouse, pencil-line black
skirt, pearls at her ears and throat—in anticipation of
seeing him.

It was that same old thing. Making him try to change
his mind. Before about kisses, now about something so
much larger.

Trust me. Let me in. Interestingly enough, not *love
me*, but *let me love you.* The most incredible thing had
happened to her over the last month, even in the face of

Ben's seeming indifference, his rejection of her. She felt better for the fact she loved him, not worse.

Beth felt deeper and more alive and more compassionate than she had ever felt. She felt like a better teacher, a better woman, a better human being. That was what love did. Genuine love didn't rip people apart, it built them up. That's what she wanted to share with Ben, this incredible truth she had discovered.

He was as handsome as ever, seemingly self-assured as he moved up the aisle past desks that seemed impossibly small.

But when he sat down on one of the adult-size chairs she had placed in front of her desk for parents, she could see his face was thinner. He looked gaunt and haunted. The plains of his handsome face were whisker-roughened, and the light had gone out in the green of his eyes.

"Are you all right?" she asked, concerned.

"Let's just keep it about Kyle," he said with rebuff.

"You look like you've been ill," she said quietly.

"Is it so hard for you to listen?" he asked.

"Is it so hard for you to realize you do not make the rules for the whole world?"

For a fraction of a second, a glimmer of a smile. Was he remembering, as she was, those long fall days of sparring with each other, how quickly the sparring could turn to laughter?

And then it was gone.

"Believe me, Beth, I know I don't make the rules for the world. No one knows that better than me."

Of course no one knew it better than him. He had buried his younger sister. And his parents. And his brothers-in-arms.

At least he'd called her Beth, leaving the door into his terrifyingly lonely world open just a crack?

That was the thing. She was not giving up on him.

"Kyle seems to be doing fairly well," she said carefully.

"Yeah. He does his homework. His report card was good."

"I wasn't talking about his homework or his report card."

"We're muddling through, Beth."

She nodded. "Peter wants him to come stay at their house for the Thanksgiving weekend. My Mom and Dad would like you both to come for Thanksgiving dinner."

"I'll ask Kyle if he wants to go. I'm sure he will. I think your mom and your nephew, Peter, are what's pulling him through this. Would you thank them for me?"

"Meaning you won't be coming for Thanksgiving dinner?"

He shook his head. "I might book a quick trip to Hawaii since Kyle will be gone."

"For four days?" she asked, incredulous.

He shrugged, his facial expressions saying he clearly didn't owe her any explanations.

"You're grieving all of it, aren't you Ben? Not just Carly? All the things that you told me you postponed."

"Don't," he said dangerously.

"Don't tell me don't," she snapped back at him. "Remember when you first came into this classroom? We were losing Kyle, and you wouldn't let it happen. You went back for him. Who's coming for you, Ben, if not me?"

"Don't you have any pride?" he snapped. "Don't waste yourself chasing after a man who doesn't want what you have to give."

The old Beth would have been felled by that arrow, but the new one stepped deftly aside, looked past the arrow to the archer.

Coming for Ben had nothing to do with her own pride, her self-esteem. In fact, it had nothing at all to do with *her*. She sensed his need and his desperation, and love as she now knew it demanded that she hang in there, hold on.

"No man left behind," she said quietly, and she felt a warrior's resolve as she said it. She was not leaving him in this prison he had made for himself. She wasn't.

He stood up so fast the chair fell over. His fists were clenching and unclenching at his sides.

"I don't want it," he said. "Do you get it? I don't want to care about anyone but myself."

"Because it hurts?" she probed softly.

"No! Because I'm self-centered and I plan to stay that way. Don't make me into something I'm not. You already invented a man once. Don't be so stupid again."

Again she watched the arrows flying at her, felt herself step out of their path, focused on him, the archer, the pain and defiance in his face.

"I'm coming for you," she said. "And you can't stop me."

He stared at her.

"I don't know if I'm coming back from Hawaii," he said.

She was sure it was a bluff, but as she contemplated saying that it didn't matter if he went to the ends of the earth, she was still coming for him, she heard the strangled gasp behind him.

When had Kyle come into the room? He stood, staring at his uncle, and then he turned on his heel and ran.

For a moment Ben's shoulders sagged and he looked nothing but defeated. "That's the kind of man I am," he said harshly. "I always seem to hurt people. That's why I don't want you coming after me, Beth."

And he turned and walked away.

The Top-Secret Diary of Kyle O. Anderson

My uncle Ben is going to Hawaii and staying there. I heard him tell Beth. I call her Beth when it's personal and Miss Maple in school. It felt weird at first but it doesn't now.

I knew something was going on with my uncle even before he said that about Hawaii. He's so quiet now. Once I saw him looking through a big book, and when he saw me, he put it away.

But I waited until he went out and went and got it. It was a photo album full of pictures of him and my mom when they were little and my grandma and grandpa when they were alive. I would have liked to look at those pictures with him, and maybe hear some of the stories of the days they were taken, but there was something in his face when he looked at them that made me afraid to ask.

For a while I thought Beth and me and him were going to be a family, but now I see it is stupid to hope for things like that. Little-kid dreams.

For a while I could pretend her family was my family. Her mom likes me to call her Bubs, just like all the grandchildren, and I call her dad Grandpa Ike. Everybody does.

Bubs sent me a card after my mom died. It is the first time I ever got mail just for me, with my name on it. She wrote in it how sorry she was. I still have it, but I think I will rip it up and throw it away.

Because as much as I like them, they aren't my family.

Uncle Ben is. I wonder if he is going to try and leave me with them. If he goes to Hawaii and stays there like I heard him tell Beth. I didn't hear him saying nothing about me going with him.

You know what? He doesn't want to care about anybody or anything.

Probably including me. So I don't want to care about anybody or anything, either. I wonder how old you have to be to join the marines? Probably not eleven.

But maybe I could join the circus.

I always was scared he wouldn't keep me. Now I know he's not going to. But I don't feel as scared as I thought I would. I feel mad.

I'm going to take Kermit and find a new place to live. I heard Australia is nice at this time of year. I bet I could stow away on a boat. Or work off my passage on a steamer.

I'm not waiting to get a postcard from Hawaii, that says, "Nice knowing you kid, have a nice life."

"Kyle?"

The house had that empty feel of when Kyle wasn't in it. Ben wondered if he had forgotten something Kyle had to do after school. Or maybe he was going to a friend's house and had forgotten to say so.

For some reason he went into Kyle's room. And frowned. The closet door was open and most of the clothes were gone. The dresser drawer also hung open, but there was nothing in it.

He looked at the fish tank where Kermit lived.

No frog.

And then he saw a note on Kyle's desk.

"Gone to Australia," it said. "Have fun in Hawaii. Bye." It was signed Kyle O. Anderson. The *O* stood for Oliver. He had been named by an orphan after an orphan. And now he was an orphan, feeling terribly alone in the world, Ben failing him at every turn.

Somehow in those words were all the pain and disappointment he had caused his nephew.

He felt the weight of his total failure. Well, what eleven-year-old didn't run away from home? When Kyle came back, hungry and tired and cold, he would tell him he hadn't really meant it about staying in Hawaii.

But he couldn't tell him the whole truth. That he'd said that just to back off Beth Maple. He didn't want her coming into the darkness to find him, even as a part of him that was weak wondered what her light could do to the darkness.

He had not been able to prepare himself for how hard it had been to see her again, her love for him, so undeserved, shining out of her eyes.

Ben shook away the compellingness of that vision and went to leave Kyle's room. But something caught his eye. Underneath the shelf that housed the empty Kermit quarters, there was a book lying on the floor.

He stooped and picked it up. It was a cheap hardbound diary with a lock on it. But it wasn't locked. In fact, it looked like it might have fallen, unnoticed, to this place.

Ben opened it to the first page, uncomfortably aware of what a breach of trust it was to read a diary. On the other hand, it might help him find Kyle.

"The Top-Secret Diary of Kyle O. Anderson," he read out loud, and felt a hint of a smile. That was Kyle. Secretive. The secrecy hiding his deep sensitivity.

Ben wasn't good with sensitivity. Another reason to let Beth go. And what about Kyle? Did he deserve something better than what his uncle could give him?

Though Ben could not even imagine giving up Kyle, not for anything. Though it was evident, after reading a few pages of that diary, that he had never managed to impress that message on his nephew.

How had he failed to make it clear to Kyle, right from the beginning, that this would be his home now? That no matter what happened, he wasn't sending him away or giving him up?

Ben had assumed Kyle knew. That stupid cowboy sheets and the surrender of his television and stereo said it all. He'd assumed. Just the way he'd assumed his sister knew he loved her. Had he ever spoken those words to his nephew? No. Here his nephew had been going to bed so scared he would not have a place to belong that his stomach hurt, and Ben had done nothing to reassure him.

No, taken away the one thing that reassured him. The growing feeling of family that they had been enjoying with Beth.

"You know what?" Ben said out loud to himself. "You have a gift for letting people down."

But the more urgent problem was where had Kyle gone? Had he cooled off before he decided to go looking for Australia? He was smarter than most eleven-year-olds, did he know getting to Australia wasn't going to be that easy?

Ben longed for Beth. For someone to turn to. But he decided to go it alone first.

Hours later, having combed every inch of Cranberry

Corner, after having talked to all the bus drivers, and gone by the train station, and hiked around Migg's Pond in the dark, there was no Kyle and no sign of Kyle.

What now? Did he call the police?

He had to talk to her. Not because she would know where Kyle was, though she might have some good ideas.

He had to talk to her because she was the one. The one who had crept by his defenses to his heart.

The one he needed to turn to with his strength failing him, when all his strength could not find that boy.

He had fallen in love with Beth Maple.

With any luck she never had to know.

Her voice was sleepy on the other end of the phone, and it warmed some part in him that was too cold. That was so damned cold.

"Beth." He said her name and he heard the way he said it. Like a benediction.

"Ben." She said his name, and he heard the way she said it, with no defenses, open to him, unafraid of the arrows.

"I'm sorry to wake you." He was aware of just how much he was sorry for.

"It's okay. What's wrong? Is it two in the morning?"

As soon as he heard her voice, everything that was muddled in him became clear. He knew where Kyle was. He knew Kyle, confused and feeling abandoned and unloved would return there.

To that place that love had grown and flourished. To a place where there had been magic in the air.

"Can you see the tree house from your bedroom window?"

"Yes."

"Would you go look at it?"

"Why?" she breathed.

Was she hoping he was inviting her, back to that magic time when they had built something together, something more than wood and concrete?

He could not let her believe that. "Kyle's missing. I think he may be there."

He could hear her moving, wondered what she was wearing, wondered what kind of man wondered something like that at a time like this.

A man unworthy, obviously.

"It's too dark," she whispered. "Do you want me to turn on the porch light?"

"No. I'll be there as soon as I can."

He parked his truck a block away so as not to spook Kyle. He walked through the darkness of inky night feeling the magic of the night, remembering. Surrendering.

She was in the yard, waiting for him, and they went up the stairs to the tree house together.

Kyle had heard them coming, and was squished back in a corner, no place to escape. "Leave me alone," he said.

Ben could clearly see that Kyle had not been prepared for the coldness of the night. His nephew was shaking.

"I'm not leaving you alone," Ben said. "Not ever."

"Yeah, sure." His sneer was forced, a child's fear right underneath it. "What about when you go to Hawaii?"

"If I went to Hawaii, permanently, you would be coming with me. You are my family."

Something relaxed fractionally in Kyle's face. "I don't want to go to Hawaii. I have friends here."

Ben contemplated that. Friends here. How a few months had changed things. And unlike him, Kyle was not damaged enough by life, even though he had every right to be, that he would run away from the gift of friendship instead of toward it.

"Okay," Ben said quietly.

"So, you're not going to Hawaii?"

"I'm not leaving you." *Say it. Tell him you love him.* But he couldn't. Were there ever words that had been spoken that were more misused than those ones? Used to manipulate? Used too casually?

Ben's mother blowing him a kiss, mouthing the words. He could not speak them, superstitious about their use.

"Come on," Beth said. "Let's go inside. I'm freezing. I need some hot chocolate." She held out an arm, and Kyle crept under it, a baby duck under her wing. He ignored Ben.

It was evident at her kitchen table that Kyle was done. His head nodded over the hot drink, his eyes kept closing, then jerking back open. But then they closed, and his head came to rest on the table, a boy utterly and completely exhausted.

"Don't wake him. Put him in the guest room," Beth said, and Ben went over and picked up his nephew.

Who was eleven years old but who felt as frail as a baby in his arms. He took him down the hall the Beth's guest room, she drew back sheets, pristine white, and he hesitated, but she was not worried about her sheets.

Always the children came first for her. Once, he had been able to picture her vividly in a wedding gown.

Now, just as vividly, he could see her like this, leaning over their children, tucking them in.

He rubbed his eyes, trying to clear the vision and the weariness that allowed such vulnerable thoughts.

"I should go," he said.

"No. We need to talk."

"Ah, the words every man dreads hearing." But somehow he didn't dread them. He needed to clear the air with her, once and for all.

"Please don't look at me like that," he said.

"Like?"

"Like you see a knight in shining armor, instead of a man of flesh and blood and bone. I am the furthest thing from that. Look at me tonight."

"What about you tonight? Your nephew was missing and you would not rest until you found him. You allowed your heart to tell you where he was."

He snorted at that. "My heart? Don't kid yourself."

"You're the one kidding yourself. I've always seen your heart. That's what I fell in love with from the very beginning."

"Don't go there."

"I don't have any choice. I feel what I feel."

"Beth," it was a cry of pure anguish, but he could not stop the words from coming. "I will let you down, just like I let down my sister. Just like I let down Kyle tonight. All she ever wanted was for me to tell her I loved her. That's all Kyle needed to hear tonight. I can't say those words. I choke on them."

"Say those words?" she said, astounded, and then she laughed softly. "Oh, you foolish, foolish man. Why would you ever have to? I *see* the love in the way you are with Kyle. Your sister had to be able to see that. I saw it the whole time you were building the tree house. Words only represent the thing. They aren't the thing. Oh, Ben, I have always seen the love pouring out of you. Always."

And then she came to him, something fierce in her

face. She took his cheeks between her hands, looked at him hard, sighed with satisfaction and welcome.

"I have always seen you," she said. "And I always will."

And then she kissed him.

And passion did not put a barrier up, because there was too much in place already for it to blur what was real.

Her passion for him took the last barrier down. It told him that she had come back for him. She had not given up until he had found his way home. To her.

The wall around his heart came down like an earthen dam after forty days and forty nights of rain. It collapsed and everything he had been holding back rushed out.

The murky, muddy water of grief, held back, churned out.

And then right behind that the cool, clean water of love. Pure love flowed out of him. And finally, finally, he said the words.

And understood that they represented not a curse but a blessing. That they represented not a prison but freedom.

The Top-Secret Diary of Kyle O. Anderson

I'm still not sure about that heaven stuff, but sometimes lately I feel my mom around me more strongly than I did when she was alive. I guess it's because I'm growing up myself that I can see all the stuff that happened to her when she was just a kid changed her. It's like a blanket got thrown over who she really was. But now the blanket is gone, and I can feel her around me, who she always should have been. I feel her when I least expect it. Like this morning we had frost, and even the weeds were covered in silver and dripped diamond droplets, like chandeliers in a mansion, and I felt her right then, something around me big and pure and sweet.

There is something around Ben and Beth like that, too. The way they look at each other, the way they touch. It's not like they run around kissing each other in front of me, but sometimes I'll just look over and see his hand cover hers and stay there, and it is like everything stops, in awe of what they have.

And they've been married two years, now. That was an awesome day. My uncle Ben asked me to be his best man. And when I saw Beth coming up the aisle looking like an angel in her long white gown, I felt like she was coming for us, not just him. And I guess she was, because me and my uncle Ben are a package deal.

Now the three of us are a package deal. I call Beth Mama B. It could be for Mama Beth, but we both know it isn't. It's for Mama Bear, because she is just like I knew she would be. Warm and fuzzy at times, but a stickler for manners and curfews, and protective of me as a mother bear with a cub. Most thirteen-year-olds would find it super annoying, but I secretly like it. Still, it will be a relief when the baby comes and she has someone else to fuss over.

Most thirteen-year-olds wouldn't like a baby coming, either. Casper and Peter both look at Beth getting rounder like it is something horrible and embarrassing, so I try not to let on how excited I feel, and happy.

This is my world and in it I feel cherished. There is room in a world like mine for a baby. Family makes everything bigger, not smaller.

My uncle is calling me. Casper is on the phone. Casper has done a lot of growing up in the past few years. He is not such a loudmouth anymore, and he never picks on me. Of course, it might help that I am an inch taller than him and outweigh him by ten pounds. Or maybe it's just that Bubs and Grandpa Ike have a swimming pool.

He wants to do our grade-seven project on Genghis Khan. I still like Genghis Khan, but not so much because he conquered the world. It is the secret side to the Khan that intrigues me.

Most people don't know he had a best friend named Jamukha, who became his blood brother. When Jamukha was elected as the universal ruler, instead of Khan, they became enemies. But when he was captured, instead of killing him, Khan, the most ruthless man who ever lived, offered a renewal of their brotherhood, which Jamukha refused.

When I was little, my uncle Ben was the most powerful man in my world. He would come to us over and over, bringing us food and gifts, and my mom was always mean to him, refusing the real gift he was bringing her, family. Love. Forgiveness.

Uncle Ben always came back, always extended the hand of a brother to her. I doubt my uncle would ever use the word *forgive*, just like he hardly ever uses the word *love*, but he forgave my mom, as if he could always see who she really was. There is something in some men that is bigger than words, that does not need words.

I know now that my mom did the best she could. I guess I could be angry at her for all the times she didn't do so great, but I'm going to be like my uncle Ben and forgive her for all the things she did do and didn't do.

I did not have a perfect childhood, but somehow it

made me a perfect me. I feel way more grown up than either Peter or Casper and like I can handle things better than them. There are things they just don't get and probably never will.

They don't get the best part of the Khan story and the most powerful part is the love he had for his brother, a love that transcended all the things that happened between them.

They don't get how wondrous toasted bread smells in the morning, or how good it feels to have five bucks in your pocket to spend on anything you like. They don't know what a good thing it is to bring a baby into the world who will have a mom and a dad and a cousin who will do anything to protect it, and who will love it no matter what it does.

Casper and Peter don't really get what it is to be afraid, what a dark place that is, like a prison. They don't really get how wonderful it is to be free, or how good that freedom can make you feel. They are both a little immature. A new TV can make them feel good.

What makes me feel good is to wait for Beth after school and we drive home together. On the way home we talk about what to make for dinner, and after I go visit with Kermit for a bit, I usually help. I'm really good at peeling potatoes, and I make the best Caesar salad.

And then my uncle comes home, and when I see the look on his face when he comes through the door, and sees us, I don't need one other thing. Not even an iPod.

He's usually all dirty and his clothes have tears in them, but Beth looks at him as if a prince has just come through the door. And then his eyes light up, and this smile comes on his face, and he picks Beth up and swings her around as if she is as light as a feather, even though she's not anymore. He swings her around until she is laughing so hard she can't stop. And then he comes and ruffles my hair and asks me about my day, and he really wants to know.

What I see in my uncle's face when he looks at Beth and me is what Genghis never knew, except maybe for one shining moment when he forgave his brother, Jamukha.

And that is that there is only one way to *really* conquer the world.

Love conquers the world. Dumb as it sounds, love really does conquer all.

Not that I'll be putting that in my grade-seven project report.

* * * * *

RICK'S APPOINTMENT with his attorney early Wednesday morning went only moderately better than his meeting with social services the day before. The prognosis wasn't great—but at least his attorney was going to file a motion for DNA testing. Just so Rick could petition to see the child…his sister's baby. The sister he didn't know he had until it was too late.

The rest of what his attorney said had been downhill from there.

Cell phone in hand before he'd even reached his Nitro, Rick punched in the speed dial number he'd programmed the day before.

Maybe foster parent Sue Bookman hadn't received his message. Or had lost his number. Maybe she didn't want to talk to him. At this point he didn't much care what she wanted.

"Hello?" She answered before the first ring was complete. And sounded breathless.

Young and breathless.

"Ms. Bookman?"

"Yes. This is Rick Kraynick, right?"

"Yes, ma'am."

"I recognized your number on caller ID," she said, her voice uneven, as though she was still engaged in whatever physical activity had her so breathless to begin with. "I'm sorry I didn't get back to you. I've been a little…distracted."

The words came in more disjointed spurts. Was she jogging?

"No problem," he said, when, in fact, he'd spent the better part of the night before watching his phone. And fretting. "Did I get you at a bad time?"

"No worse than usual," she said, adding, "Better than some. So, how can I help?"

God, if only this could be so easy. He'd ask. She'd help. And life could go well. At least for one little person in his family.

It would be a first.

"Mr. Kraynick?"

"Yes. Sorry. I was…are you sure there isn't a better time to call?"

"I'm bouncing a baby, Mr. Kraynick. It's what I do."

"Is it Carrie?" he asked quickly, his pulse racing.

"How do you know Carrie?" She sounded defensive, which wouldn't do him any good.

"I'm her uncle," he explained, "her mother's— Christy's—older brother, and I know you have her."

"I can neither confirm nor deny your allegations, Mr. Kraynick. Please call social services." She rattled off the number.

"Wait!" he said, unable to hide his urgency. "Please," he said more calmly. "Just hear me out."

"How did you find me?"

"A friend of Christy's."

"I'm sorry I can't help you, Mr. Kraynick," she said softly. "This conversation is over."

"I grew up in foster care," he said, as though that gave him some special privilege. Some insider's edge.

"Then you know you shouldn't be calling me at all."

"Yes… But Carrie is my niece," he said. "I need to see her. To know that she's okay."

"You'll have to go through social services to arrange that."

"I'm sure you know it's not as easy as it sounds. I'm a single man with no real ties and I've no intention of petitioning for custody. They aren't real eager to give me the time of day. I never even knew Carrie's mother. For all intents and purposes, our mother didn't raise either one of us. All I have going for me is half a set of genes. My lawyer's on it, but it could be weeks— months—before this is sorted out. Carrie could be adopted by then. Which would be fine, great for her, but then I'd have lost my chance. I don't want to take her. I won't hurt her. I just have to see her."

"I'm sorry, Mr. Kraynick, but…"

* * * * *

Find out if Rick Kraynick will ever have a chance to meet his niece.
Look for A DAUGHTER'S TRUST by Tara Taylor Quinn, available in September 2009.

We'll be spotlighting a different series
every month throughout 2009
to celebrate our 60th anniversary.

**Look for Harlequin® Superromance®
in September!**

*Celebrate with
The Diamond Legacy
miniseries!*

Follow the stories of four cousins as they come to terms
with the complications of love and what it means to
be a family. Discover with them the sixty-year-old secret
that rocks not one but two families.

A DAUGHTER'S TRUST by *Tara Taylor Quinn*
September

FOR THE LOVE OF FAMILY by *Kathleen O'Brien*
October

LIKE FATHER, LIKE SON by *Karina Bliss*
November

A MOTHER'S SECRET by *Janice Kay Johnson*
December

Available wherever books are sold.

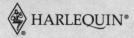

The Ranger's Secret
REBECCA WINTERS

When Yosemite Park ranger Chase Jarvis rescues
an injured passenger from a downed helicopter,
he is stunned to discover it's the woman he
once loved. But Chase is no longer the man
Annie Bower knew. Will she forgive him for
the secret he's been keeping for ten long years?
And will he forgive Annie for her own secret—
the daughter Chase didn't know he had…?

Available September
wherever books are sold.

You're invited to join our Tell Harlequin Reader Panel!

By joining our new reader panel you will:

- Receive Harlequin® books—they are FREE and yours to keep with no obligation to purchase anything!
- Participate in fun online surveys
- Exchange opinions and ideas with women just like you
- Have a say in our new book ideas and help us publish the best in women's fiction

In addition, you will have a chance to win great prizes and receive special gifts!
See Web site for details. Some conditions apply.
Space is limited.

To join, visit us at
www.TellHarlequin.com.

REQUEST YOUR FREE BOOKS!
2 FREE NOVELS PLUS 2
FREE GIFTS!

HARLEQUIN® *Romance*®

From the Heart, For the Heart

YES! Please send me 2 FREE Harlequin® Romance novels and my 2 FREE gifts (gifts are worth about $10). After receiving them, if I don't wish to receive any more books, I can return the shipping statement marked "cancel". If I don't cancel, I will receive 4 brand-new novels every month and be billed just $3.84 per book in the U.S. or $4.24 per book in Canada. That's a savings of at least 15% off the cover price! It's quite a bargain! Shipping and handling is just 50¢ per book.* I understand that accepting the 2 free books and gifts places me under no obligation to buy anything. I can always return a shipment and cancel at any time. Even if I never buy another book, the two free books and gifts are mine to keep forever.

114 HDN EYU3   314 HDN EYKG

Name	(PLEASE PRINT)
Address	Apt. #
City	State/Prov. Zip/Postal Code

Signature (if under 18, a parent or guardian must sign)

Mail to the **Harlequin Reader Service:**
IN U.S.A.: P.O. Box 1867, Buffalo, NY 14240-1867
IN CANADA: P.O. Box 609, Fort Erie, Ontario L2A 5X3

Not valid to current subscribers of Harlequin Romance books.

**Are you a subscriber of Harlequin Romance books
and want to receive the larger-print edition?
Call 1-800-873-8635 today!**

* Terms and prices subject to change without notice. Prices do not include applicable taxes. Sales tax applicable in N.Y. Canadian residents will be charged applicable provincial taxes and GST. Offer not valid in Quebec. This offer is limited to one order per household. All orders subject to approval. Credit or debit balances in a customer's account(s) may be offset by any other outstanding balance owed by or to the customer. Please allow 4 to 6 weeks for delivery. Offer available while quantities last.

Your Privacy: Harlequin Books is committed to protecting your privacy. Our Privacy Policy is available online at www.eHarlequin.com or upon request from the Reader Service. From time to time we make our lists of customers available to reputable third parties who may have a product or service of interest to you. If you would prefer we not share your name and address, please check here. ☐

HR09R

Stay up-to-date on all your romance reading news!

The Harlequin Inside Romance newsletter is a **FREE** quarterly newsletter highlighting our upcoming series releases and promotions!

Go to
eHarlequin.com/InsideRomance
or e-mail us at
InsideRomance@Harlequin.com
to sign up to receive
your **FREE** newsletter today!

HARLEQUIN *Romance*

Coming Next Month

Available September 8, 2009

This fall, curl up and relax with a Harlequin Romance® novel!

#4117 KEEPING HER BABY'S SECRET Raye Morgan
Baby on Board
Cameron's from the richest family in town. Diana's pregnant, unwed and definitely unsuitable. But will it stop these old friends from falling in love?

#4118 CLAIMED: SECRET ROYAL SON Marion Lennox
Marrying His Majesty
A year ago, Lily accidentally became pregnant with Prince Alexandros's baby. Now Alex wants to claim his son. Will Lily agree to *Marrying His Majesty?* Find out in the first book of this new trilogy!

#4119 EXPECTING MIRACLE TWINS Barbara Hannay
Follow surrogate mom Mattie's *Baby Steps to Marriage...*in the first of a new duet by Barbara Hannay. How can Mattie begin a relationship with gorgeous Jake when she's expecting twin trouble?

#4120 MEMO: THE BILLIONAIRE'S PROPOSAL Melissa McClone
9 to 5
When Chaney finds herself back working with billionaire playboy Drake, she must remember how he broke her heart, *not* his devastating charm... Oops!

#4121 A TRIP WITH THE TYCOON Nicola Marsh
Escape Around the World
Join Tamara as she travels through India on a trip of a lifetime, and catch the fireworks when she bumps into a blast from her past, maverick entrepreneur Ethan.

#4122 INVITATION TO THE BOSS'S BALL Fiona Harper
In Her Shoes...
Watch in wonder as this plain Jane is transformed from pumpkin to princess when she's hired to organize her boss's company ball...and dance in his oh-so-delicious arms!

HRCNMBPA0809